Martinis With Mom

By Dee Morgan and Lori Tucker

TABLE OF CONTENTS

CHAPTER 1
PEACH MARTINIS AT 10 AM

"I waited to open it until you got here" Jessie said to her sister. On the kitchen table sat a large envelope with *Jessie and Nicole* written in their Mother's elegant script. Bottles of vodka and peach schnapps along with two martini glasses were next to the envelope.

"It's probably just a copy of her will" Jessie said. "Or better yet, an explanation of where our mother came up with the 8 million dollars she claimed to be leaving us."

Nicole pointed to the table. "And the vodka? I suppose that's mom's way of saying Oh did I forget to mention I had millions stashed under my mattress but you have to cram yourselves into this shitty little beach hole for a year to get your hands on my money. Does she think the vodka will help take the edge off that little stipulation?"

"I don't think it's her will" Jessie said. "We already had her will read and that's pretty much why we're here."

The girls studied the envelope from a distance, and then Jessie said, "I really hope she's giving us some kind of explanation about where she got this money, like the name of the bank she must have robbed."

"Well" Nicole said, "I think we'd better make a pitcher of martinis and see what she has to say. Because unless it's a really good letter, I'm not giving up my comfy life in London to live in dear old grandma's house for a year."

"It's ten in the morning," Jessie said as she watched Nicole shake the pitcher of martinis.

"I just flew in from London," Nicole answered as she filled the two glasses. "It's four in the afternoon for me."

Jessie shook her head, knowing if she started sipping martinis at ten in the morning the rest of the day was going straight to hell. But she glanced at her sister and the envelope and decided that maybe getting blitzed was the only way to get through a day with her sister.

Jessie and Nicole settled into their chairs and propped their feet up on the railing. Nicole's curly auburn hair was matched by emerald green eyes and the delicate features that every woman dreams of. Jessie's hair was dark and straight with deep blue eyes. While their looks were completely opposite, both of the women had the same silky smooth skin that had probably never seen a blemish.

Nicole opened the large manila envelope and a stack of smaller white envelopes tumbled onto her lap. The sisters glanced at each other, and then picked up the envelopes.

"I've got a bad feeling about this, Jessie," Nicole said leafing through them. "They're numbered." She glanced at Jessie and handed her the envelope with the number one written on it. "You open it."

Jessie took a sip of her drink, placed it on the table, and took a deep breath as she opened the envelope. "Nicole," she turned to her sister "no matter what these letters say remember that our mom loved us beyond words and she has always wanted what's best for us."

"We'll see," Nicole replied. "If she wanted what's best for us, why didn't she just give us the money and forget the part about living together for a year?"

Jessie unfolded the letter and the sight of their mother's beautiful handwriting made her swallow hard before she began reading.

My Darling Daughters,

If you are reading this I have crossed over to join all of the people who I have loved and have gone before me. During my final months I spent many hours recalling my own time with my sister Gertrude. Those were among my fondest memories. I hope that you will take the time I have given you to develop some of these special memories of your own.

Each of you is so very unique but has not had the

opportunity to appreciate each other's amazing qualities. In each of these envelopes, I believe I have supplied you with a wonderful opportunity to begin to share each other's lives. Please open one envelope at the beginning of each month and complete the task at hand.

You must know from my will that there will be financial consequences for not fulfilling my wishes and while I don't mean this to sound harsh, I want to be certain that you will follow my requests. It is really quite simple, my dears: take my final wishes to your hearts and fulfill my requests, and you will become very wealthy women. If you choose to avoid the simple responsibilities I have requested, your financial future will be given to my favorite charities.

I pray that you will not resent me for insisting you spend this next year together. I know at the end of this time you will lead fuller and more meaningful lives because of each other and because of the experiences you will share. You are such unique women and I hope you can learn how to manage some of the things that life will surely hand you and in the process, learn that having a sister is one of the greatest gifts you will ever receive.

Eternal love,

Mother

Jessie and Nicole sat together in silence, sipping their drinks and trying to absorb their mother's words. "Well wasn't our mother quite the little prankster," Nicole said. "First she drops 8 million dollars on us that we knew nothing about, then she tells us we have to live together for a year to get it, and now we have to perform some kind of tasks." Nicole fingered the rest of the envelopes. "What do you think these 'wonderful opportunities' will be?"

"Whatever they are," Jessie said "Mom has just made this coming year a lot more interesting."

Later that day, the sisters decided it would be a good idea to give their Aunt Gert a call and find out if she could shed any light on all of the recent events. After all, they decided, their mother and Gert were close as sisters and if anyone knew about the 8 million dollars that was supposedly hidden away, Gert would be the one. They justified the phone call by telling themselves that they were just going to 'touch base' with their Aunt and see where the conversation led them.

Jessie went inside and dialed the number while Nicole fingered the rest of the envelopes, toying with the idea of whether or not to just burn them all and be done with it. After all, she weighed, if no one else knew about the letters and their mother's half-assed attempt at sister bonding, who would know? She was about to strike the match as Jessie broke through the doorway looking dour.

"What did Aunt Gert say?" Nicole asked.

"The long and short of it is that Aunt Gert knows about the will AND the letters." Jessie sank into the chair beside her sister.

"Oh!" Nicole slapped her thigh. "That mother of ours was more conniving than we thought. She got herself an insurance policy with Aunt Gert. Well," she glanced at Jessie "there's only one thing to do."

"What's that?" Jessie said.

"We have to kill Aunt Gert," Nicole said. "She's always been a bit on the loopy side – maybe we can slip something into her tea."

Jessie rolled her eyes at Nicole but didn't say how badly she wanted to slip something into her sister's drink at the moment.

Nicole continued acting as though taking out their aunt was a natural solution to their dilemma. "Or we'll take her out to lunch one day and just leave her there."

"We're not going to do either of those things, Nicole."

"Why not?" Nicole protested. "You read about it all the time in London. Old folks wander off and end up hundreds of miles from their home. Do you really think they just wander off?

Hell no! Some son-in-law just gets tired of listening to the old hag harp about the good old days and how she used to do things. So one day he just takes her out to lunch and she's never heard from again."

"Until she shows up on the Jerry Springer show," Jessie laughed. "Which, by the way, is where you are going to end up if you don't give up these ridiculous ideas about getting rid of Aunt Gert."

"Well then how are we going to get out of this year-long adventure our dear departed mother is sending is on?"

"I don't know," Jessie sighed "but we either need to come up with a plan B or we'll be stuck together in this shitty little beach hole – as you so fondly called our grandmother's house - for the next year."

Nicole and Jessie carried the glasses into the kitchen, and set them on the counter.

"I'll leave plan B up to you for now. I could use a hot bath and a good rest. I'm still exhausted from my traveling. Sometimes things come to me in my sleep."

"Like a vision?"

"Something like that," Nicole said, "but clearer."

"Well you go for your dreamy revelation, I'm going to unpack a few things" Jessie said as she watched Nicole leave the room. "I'll see you in a while."

As Jessie unpacked her clothes, she listened to Nicole moving around her room. She wondered how long it had been since they had actually lived in the same house, and her thoughts drifted back to their childhood. They'd been close as children, but began to grow apart as their teenage years neared. Jessie was 2 years younger and wanted nothing more than to spend her time with the 4-H club. Nicole became obsessed with shopping for the latest styles in clothes and makeup and Jessie wondered what would have become of her sister had their family not had the luxury of wealth.

As they grew older, the distance between them became obvious to their family and when Nicole moved to London, there seemed to be less and less to talk about on their phone calls. Eventually, they called each other only on their birthdays and Christmas. Jessie thought about having to live with Nicole for the next year. It would be a difficult experience. Nicole was a good person with a quick wit, but her sarcasm could be tiresome. Jessie's calm, practical demeanor was the polar opposite of Nicole's outgoing flamboyancy and she knew it would take a boatload of patience to get through most days.

Jessie sighed as she heard Nicole bellowing an old Beatles song while she soaked in the tub. Mother, she said to herself, I guess this whole thing seemed like a good idea to you at the time.

The following morning Nicole found Jessie sipping a cup of coffee and reading the paper. "Any brilliant dreams?" Jessie asked.

"Actually, yes" Nicole answered. "I have the perfect solution to our situation."

Jessie looked at Nicole as she settled into her chair. "Really," she said. "Have you found a more devious way to get rid of Aunt Gert?"

"We don't have to get rid of her," Nicole said. "We can bribe her."

"This came to you in your sleep?"

"Yes," Nicole answered. "We can each offer her a hundred thousand dollars to keep her old trap shut."

"Nicole!" Jessie said. "You cannot seriously think that Aunt Gert would take a bribe to cover up our deceit?"

"I would," she answered, looking wounded.

"Do you even remember Aunt Gert?" Jessie asked.

"I remember she was always a bit quirky. She used to tie her hair up in little red and yellow rags. It made her look like a miniature version of Mt. St. Helens spewing lava down the sides of her head."

Jessie laughed, "Well, I still don't think she'd take a bribe."

"We won't know unless we ask, will we?" Nicole urged.

Jessie pondered her sister's plan as she sipped her coffee. "Okay," she finally said. "But we can't call it a bribe."

"Fine," Nicole agreed. "Let's just say we need her cooperation and we'll make it worth her while."

"Oh great," Jessie smirked. "That sounds like something from an old gangster movie. Can't we just explain that we can't take a year off from our lives and if we had the money from mother, we'd be more than happy to enhance her financial security?"

"Sounds like a bribe to me," Nicole said.

"Well then what do you think we say to her?" Jessie asked.

"I guess you're right. Let's just come clean with her and promise to mail her a bucket of money."

"Great," Jessie agreed. "I'll call her but you have to stay right by my side. I'll put her on speaker phone," Jessie said as she dialed the phone.

Jessie and Nicole looked at each other, "Hello, Aunt Gert," Jessie said. "How are you this morning?"

"What are you girls up to?" Aunt Gert snapped. "I just talked to you last night so you know how I am."

"Uh...well, Nicole and I had something we wanted to propose to you," Jessie stammered.

"You have to do what your Mother wants you to do," Aunt Gert blurted. "It was her last wishes. Didn't you girls disappoint her enough when she was alive? You want to somehow skirt around her dying wishes?"

Jessie and Nicole felt chastised next to Aunt Gert's words and surprised that she had so quickly surmised what their plan was going to be.

"No," Jessie tried to recover. "What we wanted to propose is that we get together sometime soon."

"Sure." Aunt Gert's voice reminded Jessie of where Nicole's sarcastic tone had originated. "And I wanted to propose that Prince Charles come over for dinner next week and bring that hag of a wife with him."

Jessie and Nicole stayed silent, realizing their Aunt Gert

was many things, but naïve wasn't among them. "When do you want to come?" she suddenly asked, softening her tone. "I have my drama club tomorrow, my bowling league day after."

Jessie seemed unable to collect her thoughts. "Why don't you call us when you have some time."

"That went well" Nicole smirked when they'd hung up the phone. "She thinks we're a couple of disappointing women who wouldn't respect our mother's last wishes."

Jessie glanced at her sister. "That's exactly what we are. We're trying to concoct some story to convince our old aunt that our lives are too busy and too important to honor our mother's wishes, and when that doesn't work, we're willing to bribe her." Jessie shook her head. "To be honest about it, Nicole, what we're thinking really is quite shameful."

Nicole riled at her sister's remarks. "So what you're saying is because I don't want to give up my life in London for a year, that I'm a dreadful person?"

Jessie was beginning to grow tired of Nicole's defensive attitude and it came out in her words. "You know, this whole situation isn't all about you, Nicole. Mother didn't request that <u>you</u> give up a year of <u>your life</u>, she said that <u>we</u> should give up a year of <u>our lives</u>." Jessie paused for a breath before she continued. "And it's not like we're doing this for nothing. There's a pot of gold waiting for us, so put on your big girl panties and let's just get on with it. We don't have to like each other, but we do need to get through this next year without killing Aunt Gert or each other."

Nicole stood stunned for a moment at Jessie's words, then turned on her heel and walked to her bedroom. Well, Jessie thought, I'm not sure I can get through the next hour without strangling her, much less a year.

Mother, she sighed, what were you thinking?

CHAPTER 2
PERSONAL SHOPPING FOR HORSE SHOES

Nicole waited a full hour before emerging from her room. Jessie seemed to be nowhere around, but her car was in the drive so Nicole knew she couldn't have gone far. She stepped onto the deck and scanned the beach where she saw the two dogs, Gus and Higgins, jumping happily around each other, followed by Jessie walking slowly toward the house.

I guess she's right, Nicole thought to herself. We're both going to have to make a sacrifice and I suppose compared to some of the sacrifices mother must have made, we should be ashamed of ourselves.

Gus and Higgins came bounding up the steps toward Nicole. Higgins was wearing his yellow shirt that read "Don't Try Me" and Gus was shaking the sand from his snout.

"It was really nice walking today," Jessie said. "Cold, but a pretty day."

"I'm really sorry about earlier," Nicole said. "Sometimes I get a bit self-absorbed and need someone to reel me in."

"Look," Jessie said "maybe I was bit harsh with what I said to you."

"No," Nicole sighed, "you weren't. But we do need to decide what we're going to do."

Jessie leaned against the railing, the breeze coming off the ocean hitting her back. "The way I see it," she said, "the only thing we can do is to honor mother's will."

Nicole glanced at her sister and nodded. "I know you're right, but my God, Jessie. A whole year? And who knows what mother has in store for us in those little white envelopes. I feel like I'm being sent to prison for a year and don't know what my crime has been."

Jessie raised her eyebrows and smiled. "Surely I'm not that bad."

Nicole shook her head and smiled. "That's not what I meant. We just don't know what is going to be in those envelopes."

"We'll find out soon enough but before we do, how about if we take a ride out to the ranch tomorrow? You haven't been there in a long time and I've done a lot of work with it. Besides," she added, "I need to show you that I don't grow beans, I run a horse rescue ranch."

"Oh, not fair!" Nicole stamped her foot. "We get to visit your ranch but I can't drive off and visit London for the day."

"Yeah," Jessie laughed as she stepped into the house. "Life's a bitch."

The ride to the ranch the following day proved to be pleasant enough for the two women who were crossed between sisters and strangers. They got on famously one minute and the next were already tiring of their time together. Their conversation was casual at best and strained during the better part of the ride.

Nicole talked about how much she was going to miss all of her clients as well as the fabulous shopping trips to design houses that she was paid extremely well to visit.

"So people actually pay you to buy their clothes" Jessie marveled. "Why would they do that?"

"Lots of reasons" Nicole explained. "Sometimes they know their taste in fashion borders on hideous and they'd rather trust a personal shopper like me. Other times, they're so busy planning their next charity event their calendar doesn't allow time for shopping."

"I don't have a lot of spare time either" Jessie laughed "but I never considered hiring someone to buy my clothes."

"Luckily" Nicole said as she re-tied her scarf, "not everyone thinks like you do or else I'd be out of a job."

"What about your clients?" Her sister's profession intrigued Jessie. "Are they hard to please?"

"Oh, some of them have egos that are a bit inflated and they can get a bit difficult, but usually I spend enough time with a client to understand what they need."

Jessie laughed again, then said, "One thing about horses, Nicole, is that they don't have an ego."

"True" Nicole agreed "but they also don't wear $4000 gowns, of which I get a very nice commission."

Nicole looked around and noticed how the landscape had changed from the distinct look and feel of a beach community to the peaceful countryside with acres of lush green fields. She studied her sister's face as Jessie drove and noticed that – like the scenery – her features had also changed. She looked relieved to be coming back to the ranch, even if it was only for a few hours.

"I guess what you do is important to you" Nicole offered.

"It is" Jessie answered, dismissing Nicole's attempt at a compliment. "The rescue ranch has given me a lot of pleasure since I quit the farming thing."

Nicole grimaced as she looked quickly at Jessie. "I guess I owe you an apology for the farm remark the other day. It's just that I didn't understand that you own a ranch, not a farm."

Jessie glanced at her sister, whose mane of red hair was being held captive beneath a fashionable winter scarf. "Tell me" Jessie pressed, "is it because you think I look like a farmer? Because I've never wanted to be the fashion plate that you are, Nicole. I'm perfectly comfortable in a pair of jeans but believe it or not, I do clean up rather nicely."

"Seriously, I apologize." Nicole tried to continue on but Jessie stopped her.

"I know your looks are important in your line of work, but when I'm knee deep in hay and horse shit, the color of my lipstick isn't really on the top of my list."

Nicole laughed and then let it drop. "Jessie" Nicole turned in her seat "what do you know about this eight million dollars that mother claims to have had in her will?"

Jessie shook her head slowly. "I was as shocked as you were. I knew mother never worried about money, but I always assumed that she had dad's life insurance and stocks, just like we have."

"No" Nicole said. "Grandpa and Dad made sure we were always taken care of, but I don't believe they had that much in stocks."

"Where do you think it came from then?"

"I don't know" Nicole said. "You saw mother much more often than I did. Can you think of anything that might explain eight million dollars?"

Jessie thought hard for a few minutes. "I don't know," she said. "Mother used to travel a lot, especially the last few years. Sometimes she'd refer to a friend that she visited, but nothing specific."

"A friend?" Nicole was intrigued. "As in a male friend?"

"I don't think so" Jessie said "but I can't remember the name."

"Oh think," Nicole pleaded. "This could be a huge hint."

"I had always assumed it was a woman," Jessie observed.

"Did you ever meet her?"

"No, but I was certain it was just a woman friend." Jessie tried to recall any particular trip that her mother had talked about, any hint that Jessie may have missed.

"What makes you so sure it's a woman?"

Jessie thought for a moment then said, "I guess because I never considered the idea that mother would have a boyfriend and we wouldn't know anything about it."

"We've got to find out more about this money" Nicole said, already convinced that something sinister was in the wind for them.

Jessie swung the car up the long drive toward her house. Nicole looked over the pasture at the array of horses that stood there. Some stood two or three together, as if they were exchanging the latest gossip, while others stood alone, still as a statue. "How many horses do you have?" Nicole asked.

"Last I knew there were just ten."

"Last you knew?" Nicole asked with a puzzled grin. "Don't you own this place?"

"Yes" Jessie smiled "but Jake and his staff actually take care of things. I pretty much make the decisions when it comes to spending the money and signing the checks. Other than that, Jake is the man."

Nicole watched as a tall, dark haired man strode toward the house and Nicole could see he had a body that was well toned from hard work. "And," Nicole pulled down her sunglasses "would that fine specimen be Jake?"

Jessie waved as she pulled to a stop in front of the house.

"That would be Jake," she smiled.

Nicole slid off her sunglasses never taking her eyes off Jake who was walking towards the car. "I don't recall you ever mentioning this Jake guy," Nicole said as she checked her lipstick in the mirror.

"There's nothing to mention. He works for me, runs the place, end of story" Jessie said.

Nicole smiled. "You go ahead and tell yourself that, little sister, but I know better. We may not be the bare your soul kind of friends like some people, but we're still sisters, and as far as I can tell, we're both still single and breathing. I'd be all over that cowboy if I were you."

"Nicole, hush" Jessie whispered. "He'll hear you." Jake reached down and pulled open the door for Jessie and gave her a gentle hug.

"Hey Jess," he said. "You look pretty today."

Just friends, my ass, Nicole thought to herself. Who the hell is she kidding? Nicole reached for the door handle but before she could push it Jake had opened it and extended his hand for her.

"Hi, you must be Nicole" Jake said as he helped her out of the car. "I'm Jake, glad to finally meet you."

"Likewise" Nicole smiled.

"Jessie has told me a lot about you. I'm guessing that Pawley's Island must seem pretty boring compared to London" Jake asked as he walked over and stood behind Jessie.

"One would think, but mommy dearest must have been experimenting with her meds when she was drawing up her will." Nicole glanced over to her sister. "So here I am, 2 days down, 363 to go."

"Not that she's counting" Jessie laughed.

"She's exactly as you described her." Jake put his hands on Jessie's shoulders.

"Oh really," Nicole asked. "Just how did my sister describe me? Do tell."

"Funny and beautiful" Jake answered quickly.

"Wow, good looking and charming," Nicole laughed. "Jessie, honey, you should really marry this guy before he gets away."

"Nicole! That's enough!" Jessie turned to face Jake. "She's just kidding, Jake. She's like a five-year old - never know what's going to come out of that mouth of hers."

Nicole seemed amused at her sister's obvious discomfort

but decided to let it drop for the moment. They headed toward the house down a walkway lined in gardenia and jasmine and when Nicole stopped to take a deep breathe of the aroma that permeated the cool morning air, memories of her childhood in South Carolina came rushing back. She hadn't realized until that very moment how much she had missed it here.

Nicole's thoughts were interrupted by the smell of fresh baked pie as they entered the kitchen. "Oh my God" she said as she inhaled deeply. "What is that wonderful smell?"

"Miss Nell bakes a mean apple pie," Jake offered. "Hard to resist."

"Who said anything about resisting?" Nicole laughed.

"I think we should have lunch before we tackle that pie," Jessie said. "I think Miss Nell put some chicken salad in the fridge for us."

"Yes I did," a voice boomed from the doorway, "and y'all just settle down while I fix up a nice lunch."

Jessie hugged her housekeeper, introduced her to Nicole, and smiled again at Jake. Nicole noticed how easily Jake fit into the house and she wondered once again how her sister, who was a dark haired beauty herself, had managed to keep her hands off her cowboy ranch manager.

Over lunch Nicole tried discreetly to study Jake and Jessie. They're perfect together, she thought. Jake managed to be reserved but confident at the same time. Jessie's blue eyes sparkled when she talked about the horses, but lit up the room when she looked at Jake. Could she be lying to me? Nicole wondered. There's no way these two aren't in love with each other. I don't care what they say or how many ways they try to deny it. If they haven't done the deed yet, a roll in the hay can't be far off.

"Miss Nell," Nicole smiled "that was a wonderful lunch. That pie was just pure heaven. Thank you."

"Well, darlin' it was my pleasure," the housekeeper drawled. "Now I want y'all to git so I can put this kitchen back in order."

They left the house and walked toward the barn with Jake between Jessie and Nicole, although Nicole noticed he walked just a bit closer to Jessie.

"I think Sailor has a problem with his legs" Jake was telling Jessie. "I noticed it last week and I've been keeping an eye on him. He may need some special shoes."

Nicole stopped in her tracks. "Special shoes? Are you kidding me? Do they have orthopedic shoes for horses?" she joked.

"Actually they do" Jessie answered.

Nicole hooted with laughter. "That's the wildest thing I ever heard," she howled. "Who makes these things? Surely not Jimmy Choo." Jake and Jessie laughed out loud at Nicole's antics as she continued. "What do they look like? Do they have special laces up the front and extra support in their arches?"

"Nicole," Jessie laughed, "calm down. They're horse shoes, not people shoes."

"Oh thank God" Nicole laughed. "I thought I was going to have to put a new spin on my career as a personal shopper for horses. I'd have to make some calls to the Wildlife Society to find out who the top designers are for orthopedic horse shoes."

Jessie and Jake gave Nicole the full tour of the ranch, from the house to the barn to the ranch house where most of the ranch hands lived. Nicole noticed that Jake had his own place but decided to leave that bit of information alone for the moment.

"I guess what I do seems kind of silly compared to saving horses," Nicole said after they arrived back at the house.

"Do you enjoy what you do for a living?" Jessie asked.

"Oh I love it," Nicole said happily. "I love following the new fashions, and seeing the look on women's faces when they see how lovely they can look in what I've chosen."

"Well there you go" Jessie said. "I make horses happy and you make people happy. It doesn't seem so silly to me."

Nicole glanced over at her sister. "Thanks" she said. "And thanks for the tour of the ranch."

"My pleasure" Jessie said. "We'd better start back to Pawley's Island," she said as she pulled out her keys.

"What about Jake?" Nicole blurted. Jessie looked at her sister, puzzled for a moment at her question. "What about him?"

"I didn't get to say goodbye to him," Nicole answered. "I don't know when I'll see him again."

Jessie studied Nicole's face. "We'll drive by the barn on the way out."

"I'll tell you one thing" Nicole smiled as she settled into the car. "For someone who spends all that time in a barn with hay and horses, that Jake sure smells good."

Jessie gave her sister a sidelong glance and drove to the barn. Jake walked toward the car and smiled as Jessie stepped from the car to greet him.

"We're heading back to the beach," Jessie said to him. "We

just wanted to say goodbye and see if there was anything else you needed from me."

Jake put his hands on Jessie's shoulders and lowered his voice. "You really want me to answer that?" he smiled. Jessie felt her face flush a bit, knowing the meaning behind the words.

"Jake" she said softly "I'll miss you."

"It doesn't have to be this way between us, Jess." Jessie had expected this reaction from Jake but his gentle determination was making her denials more difficult to justify. Jake knew exactly how Jessie felt about him and had respected her resistance but had never fully accepted it.

"It does for now, Jake. Please understand." He slid his arms from her shoulders, disappointment clouding his eyes.

"Call me" was all he said to her.

"I'll check with you every few days. And" she poked her finger playfully at Jake's chest "you'd better call me if anything comes up."

"Sure" he smiled and leaned in to the car toward Nicole. "It was a pleasure to meet you, Nicole."

"Likewise" she smiled. "And I'm sure I'll be seeing you again."

The girls headed off the Pawley's and by the time they got to the house, both decided they were too exhausted for even their peach martini nightcap.

At 3:00 AM, Jessie awoke to find Nicole poking her. "Wake up. I had a dream."

"Nicole," Jessie moaned, "what could possibly be so important that it couldn't wait until morning."

"The money" she said. "The eight million dollars!"

Jessie raised herself up on her elbow. "What about it?"

"I dreamed about Aunt Gert" Nicole said.

"What about Aunt Gert?"

"Well if Aunt Gert knows about the letters, and she knows about the will"

"She must know about the money," they said in unison.

"Nicole," Jessie smiled, "there might be something to these dreams of yours after all."

The following morning, Jessie and Nicole were at the table planning a visit to Aunt Gert.

"This was brilliant" Jessie said. "If we promise Aunt Gert that we're going to do whatever mother put in those letters, why wouldn't she tell us where the money came from?"

"Because she's mean and ornery?" Nicole quipped.

"She's not mean," Jessie said. "She just hasn't always had things go her way."

"That's because she kept running off her husbands" Nicole answered. "How many times has she been married?"

"I think just three."

"Well, that's three more husbands than either one of us has landed" Nicole said. Jessie let the remark go and said, "We have to go see Aunt Gert if we're going to find out about the money. You call her this time."

"Oh no," Nicole backed away. "I don't have near the gift that you do. If she starts going on with me, I'll probably just piss her off and then we won't get any information from her. No…you should call her. You're much better at this kind of thing than I am." Nicole paused then realized she hadn't yet convinced her sister that Jessie was the best one for this job. "Besides" she added, "I haven't talked to Aunt Gert in years. How can I just call up and say 'Hi, we want to visit and pump you for information about our mother's fortune.' That wouldn't be very nice."

Jessie tapped her fingers on the table. "Fine. But you'd better help me decide what we're going to say. You'd better not leave all the talking up to me."

The following day, they stood nervously on Aunt Gert's front porch. Nicole glanced around and poked Jessie. "Why are there bowling balls in her garden?"

Jessie looked past Nicole and saw six brightly colored bowling balls planted along the front of the house. Before she could answer, the door swung open and Aunt Gert smiled broadly.

"Well look at you," she said. "Come in, come in" and smiled at the sisters and gave each one a quick hug. The house was small and cozy and just as neat as Nicole had remembered. Aunt Gert hadn't changed much either – her hair a little whiter and shorter, her waist a little thicker, but basically Aunt Gert was the same feisty woman she'd been the last time Nicole had visited her.

"You look wonderful, Aunt Gert" Nicole said. "You must be taking good care of yourself."

Aunt Gert looked at her, not understanding why Nicole would say such a thing. "Of course I take care of myself" she finally offered. "Got rid of that no good husband of mine so I have no one else I need to worry about."

Nicole and Jessie both smiled a bit lamely as they stood in the hallway, not knowing whether to invite themselves to sit down, or wait for Aunt Gert to make the offer.

"I made us some muffins," Aunt Gert finally offered. If she'd been aware of the sister's awkwardness, she didn't give a hint to it. "We'll have some tea and a nice visit."

Nicole had always thought Aunt Gert was one of the strangest women she'd ever met. So far, this visit did nothing to dispel the idea. She was curious about the colored bowling balls in the garden, but thought she'd better restrain herself from asking. The slight tension in the air was cut when they sat at the table and Aunt Gert began to reminisce about their mother. It was the opening Jessie and Nicole had been waiting for.

"Your mother always loved these muffins" Aunt Gert started. "She'd come over to visit in the mornings, on her way to wherever she was off to that day. We'd sit and talk about everything. Of course" Aunt Gert laughed "her life was much more interesting than mine, but some days we'd spend hours just sitting here until every one of these muffins was gone and we'd solved all of the world's problems."

Jessie was beside herself to jump at the chance. "Why do you say mother's life was more interesting than yours?"

Aunt Gert eyed Jessie skeptically and said, "Because it was, that's why."

Nicole fidgeted for a moment in her chair then said "Aunt Gert, it was a long ride – could I use your bathroom?"

"It's where it always was, Nicole. Down the hall to the right."

Jessie wanted to throttle her sister. The ride over here took all of one hour and Nicole had spent enough time in the bathroom before they left to use the facilities ten times.

Jessie took a chance and gently pressed Aunt Gert. "I always thought your life was pretty special," she said. "Mother may have traveled more than you, but that was your choice wasn't it?"

Aunt Gert softened a bit. "Never wanted to leave my little piece of heaven here, Jessie. I didn't see the need. Everything I want is right here in Charleston. Your mother, however, had people and places she wanted to see."

"People?" Jessie asked. Aunt Gert looked at Jessie but she couldn't read her Aunt's eyes. "Aunt Gert" she finally said quietly "did my mother have someone else in her life?"

"Well" Aunt Gert said slowly "I know you'd like an answer to that, so I'll give you one." Jessie's heart raced and she hoped that Nicole didn't come blasting back into the room and ruin the moment.

"Yes" Aunt Gert offered, "your mother had someone very special in her life." Jessie waited for her Aunt to continue but the only thing she said was "Would you like me to warm that tea for you?"

"Aunt Gert" Jessie pleaded "what can you tell me about him?" Nicole must have heard the conversation because she returned to the kitchen and slipped quietly into her chair.

"I can tell you lots about him," she said, "but I'm not going to." Jessie and Nicole glanced at each other and frowned.

"Why not?" Nicole asked.

"Well" Aunt Gert started "for one thing, if my sister wanted you girls in her business, she'd have let you in. For another" she stood and walked toward the stove "he's dead. Let him rest."

"Well, that's not very fair" Nicole said. "If they're both dead, what harm could it do to tell us about him?"

"Nicole" her Aunt said firmly "you've always been the pushy one. Well let me tell you a little secret, missy. I can't be pushed. Three husbands have tried. Didn't work with them –

won't work with you."

"Nicole," Jessie said, "we have to respect Aunt Gert. If she doesn't want us to know about mother's lover, then so be it."

Nicole looked puzzled at her sister. "But" she started and Jessie put up her hand.

"Aunt Gert" Jessie said "is there nothing you can tell us? Nothing that would help us understand this whole thing? Mother had eight million dollars and we don't have a clue where it came from."

Their Aunt had her back to them at the counter and the girls weren't certain she had even heard them.

"Is that where our mother got the money?" Nicole asked. "From this mystery man?"

Aunt Gert turned to face them and her features seemed to soften as she spoke. "Everything you need to know," she said, "you will find at your grandmother's house and in Charleston. Now" she sat at the table "no more about this. Tell me what you both have been up to in your lives. And why aren't either one of you married?" And, it seemed to Jessie and Nicole, the subject of their mother, her mysterious lover, and the eight million dollars was now closed.

After several hours, Aunt Gert knew all there was to know about Jessie and Nicole's lives, the colored bowling balls had been explained, and the story of Aunt Gert's three husbands had been told.

"So" Nicole said on the drive back to the house, "that's it? We're not going to make Aunt Gert tell us anything else?"

"What did you want me to do, Nicole, beat it out of her?"

"No, but you could have pressed her a little harder" Nicole said.

"And I didn't see you offering to jump in and pump some information out of her." Jessie was less angry than she sounded but it had been a frustrating visit with their aunt and it seemed they had gotten nothing except a confirmation that their mother indeed had a lover, and a reminder that neither of them had found a man that would tolerate them.

Nicole opted to let that remark slide, mostly because she knew Jessie had a valid point.

"What do you think she meant that everything we need to know is either at the house or in Charleston?"

"Hmmm" Jessie said as she pulled the car into the drive. "I think we'd better make a trip to the attic. Mother stored a lot of things up there. Who knows what we might find."

"Ooohhh" Nicole's eyes lit up. "A treasure hunt. Let's go."

Jessie and Nicole dropped their purses in the hallway and headed up the narrow stairway that led to the attic. The light was dim but the layers of dust were plainly visible. "I don't think anyone has been up here in years" Jessie commented as she climbed across the floor to make room for Nicole.

"Why don't you pull out a few boxes and I'll carry them down?" Nicole offered.

Jessie gave her sister a sidelong glance. "Nice try" she said, "but if I have to be up here, so do you."

"Oh alright" Nicole agreed. "But there'd better not be any rats up here."

The sisters spent the next hour separating boxes, their mother's in one area, and their grandmother's in another. The huge trunk in the middle of the room, they decided, would have to stay put. They could go through that when the light was a little better. They agreed their mother's boxes would probably offer the most information, and as they carried the last of them downstairs, they were surprised to see it was nearly midnight.

"I think we'd better start this in the morning" Nicole said. "I'm exhausted."

"We'll get up early," Jessie added. "I can't wait to see what secrets are in some of these boxes."

"Speaking of secrets" Nicole said as they piled the last of the boxes in the hallway, "I just don't get you and this guy Jake. What's the real story there?"

Jessie smiled but offered nothing, saying only "Let's solve one mystery at a time."

As Jessie climbed into bed she began to think about her situation with Jake. She wouldn't tell Nicole anything for several reasons. First, she knew that while they would obviously be living together for the next year, she didn't think she and Nicole would ever develop the closeness their mother had shared with her sister Gert. But more than that, Jessie knew there wasn't much to tell Nicole about her and Jake. Their relationship seemed so complicated that even if Jessie opted to share anything with Nicole, she wasn't sure she would know where to begin. She had so many feelings for Jake, and she knew he felt the same way. They'd actually talked about it over dinner one evening just after her mother had gotten ill, but Jessie had told Jake that she thought the wisest move for both of them was to maintain their friendship. She was, after all, his boss. If they moved into a more personal relationship and things didn't work out, Jake would be out of a job and Jessie would be out of a ranch manager.

Jessie recalled the deep disappointment that filled Jake's

eyes that night, and the questions that now filled her days about her decision. She played the 'what if' scenarios so many times night after night that she had come close to calling him several times to say she'd changed her mind. And as sleep began to move across her mind, Jessie thought about the tender kisses they had shared that same night. She thought about how Jake had whispered her name and said 'Are you sure, Jess?' And she recalled how it took every bit of self-control for her to pull back and tell him yes, this is the best way...the only way.

Jessie hadn't seen Jake for weeks after that night. She spent the majority of her time at Pawley's taking care of her mother and while she spoke to Jake almost every day, their conversations were short and centered around the ranch. It was several weeks before Jake asked her when she planned on coming by the ranch and Jessie recalled the elation she felt thinking he missed her. But in the end, there were papers that needed to be signed and Jake said he would mail them to her. She hung up the phone feeling completely dispirited. She left her mother with Gert that day and drove to town, simply to be alone and reflect on the result of her own decision.

Jessie fell asleep still reflecting on her words to Jake that night.

CHAPTER 4
WHO SAYS YOU CAN'T EAT CHEETOS FOR BREAKFAST

Early the next morning, Nicole and Jessie started going through the boxes. They were anxious to know about the millions their mother claimed to have. They knew they'd get nothing out of the attorney and even less out of Aunt Gert. They had slid into a peaceful tolerance of each other, neither anxious to deal with the envelopes their mother had left for them. Their new project was just the diversion they were looking for and they attacked it with gusto.

After 2 days of sorting through the first batch of boxes, Nicole and Jessie had become so absorbed in looking for the slightest hint of who their mother's lover was and where she had come upon eight million dollars, that their eating habits became secondary. They had fallen into a routine of Cheerios for breakfast, Oreos for lunch, and martinis for dinner over a delicate array of Nachos, Doritos, Cheetos, and the proper accompanying dips. They called it the O diet – any food ending in O seemed to be acceptable cuisine.

"Jessie," Nicole said, "we've been doing this for two straight days and haven't found a single thing that tells us anything about mother's secret life."

"I know" Jessie agreed. "There must be more boxes somewhere else with everything we're looking for."

"Well, I'm not going back into that filthy attic" Nicole pouted. "I sneezed all night long from that dust."

Ignoring Nicole's pouting, Jessie coaxed her sister with "I'll bet there's tons of stuff in that old chest up there."

Nicole eyed Jessie. "Okay," she relented, "but there better be some juicy stuff up there or else I'm going to go back to Aunt Gert and choke the details out of her." Moments later they were opening the chest and as Jessie rummaged through the old clothes and hats, she dug beneath and came up with a small locked box.

"Nicole" she exclaimed. "Look...this must be it."

Nicole held up the envelope she had in her hand and said "This too, Jess. It's a bunch of old love letters. And since our father's name wasn't Garrett, I believe we've hit the jackpot."

"You've got letters" Jessie scrambled over to where Nicole sat "and this box is locked. What could she want to hide that was more personal than love letters?"

"Pictures!" the girls chimed. "Is there a key?" Nicole asked as Jessie crawled back to the chest.

"I don't find one," she said as she dug through the chest.

"Break it open," Nicole said. "We're entitled to know what

mother was hiding from us."

The sisters climbed back down to the kitchen and Jessie fumbled through the drawer and came up with a screwdriver. In a matter of moments, they dumped the contents onto the kitchen table. Jessie and Nicole combed through the photos, marveling at the fact that their mother had an entire life neither had known about.

"Read me some of the letters," Jessie urged. "Pictures are good, but they don't explain anything." The sisters sat for hours taking turns looking at pictures and reading the letters.

"Nicole" Jessie finally said "don't you feel a bit...I don't know," she paused and then continued. "It just feels wrong to be reading their private thoughts and feelings."

Nicole folded the letter she was holding and placed it on the table. She smiled at Jessie and spoke softly. "It does feel awkward, but how else are we going to find out about Garrett? And where mother got all of this money? Besides" she poked Jessie's arm "if mother didn't want us to know about him, why didn't she burn these letters and pictures?"

Jessie was surprised at Nicole's rare display of common sense and sat thoughtful for a moment. "I suppose you're right" she said. "Mother must have known that we would eventually go through the attic."

"See?" Nicole said. "I knew we would finally agree on something."

Jessie smiled and turned back to leafing through the photos, stopping suddenly to study one in particular. She turned it over and written on the back in their mother's script, she read "June 20, 2006".

"Nicole, look at this. What does this look like?"

Nicole snatched the photo from Jessie and studied it front and back. She looked quickly from the photo to Jessie and back to the photo." This looks like a wedding picture" Nicole said. "Did they get married?"

"I don't know."

"Well" Nicole said, "I've had about all of this mystery I can take." She stood and marched to the phone. "I'm calling that seedy attorney to demand he tell us the whole story."

Jessie studied her sister for a moment. "I have to agree with you. Maybe Mr. Justice will be willing to clear this up for us."

Two days later, Jessie and Nicole sat in front of Jethro A. "Sonny" Justice. "Well," he drawled, "I can't say I was surprised by your call."

"Look," Nicole was determined to get every bit of information she could.

Jessie placed her hand gently on her sister's arm. "Mr. Justice," Jessie spoke with more reserve, "our mother seems to have had a life outside of the one we knew."

The attorney looked from one sister to the other. "Yes" he said finally. "Indeed she did."

"I knew it" Nicole said. "She was married to this Garrett person, wasn't she?"

"Nicole" Jessie said sharply. "Let Mr. Justice finish."

Nicole leaned back in her chair but added, "We want to know everything." Jessie thought she sounded like a hard-nosed detective from a TV show.

The attorney sat forward and began to speak. "First of all, yes, your mother and Garrett were wed shortly after your father passed away."

"Yes" Nicole interrupted again "like six months after daddy died."

Ignoring her sister, Jessie asked, "Why didn't she tell us?"

Jethro sighed, "Your mother was a complicated woman."

"Continue" Nicole said curtly. Jessie gave her sister a stern look but said nothing.

The attorney shuffled some papers as he began to speak. "Before your mother and Garret decided to marry, they already knew he was terminally ill. Garrett was a very wealthy man and he wanted to ensure that your mother received everything he wanted her to have. Had they not wed, there might have been some" he paused and tapped his fingers together. "Well, there may have been some associates that could have contested his will. They would have lost, of course, but things could have been tied up in the courts for quite some time. With your mother as his wife, the likelihood that his will would have been contested was greatly diminished."

Jethro stopped and waited for the sisters to absorb this news and to ask the inevitable questions.

"It still doesn't explain why she didn't want Nicole and me to know."

Jethro sighed loudly. "That, I'm afraid, I cannot completely answer. Your mother," he smiled "would only say that she loved your father deeply and always would, and she did not want her daughters to ever doubt that fact."

"Did she love Garrett?" Nicole asked, finally calming to the situation.

"Of course" the lawyer said. "Garrett was a wonderful man. He loved your mother from the moment he met her."

"And" Nicole's tone had softened "when exactly was that moment?"

"Your mother and Garrett met in 2004. They were both very involved with the Pet Rescue project and" he held up his hands "before you ask, I can assure you that while the attraction was strong between them, your mother was faithful to your father to the very end."

"And is this where mother got eight million dollars to leave to us?" Jessie asked.

Jethro nodded. "And before your mother passed, she also gave her sister Gert quite a generous gift, along with" The attorney stopped short, as though he had come close to giving away some information that was better left unsaid. "Gert had a fit about getting so much money," he continued, "and to tell you the truth, I don't think she has touched a penny of it yet."

Jessie noticed that the attorney suddenly seemed uncomfortable with the discussion, but Nicole seemed not to notice.

"Hmph" Nicole snorted "I'll bet Aunt Gert doesn't have a pile of letters that say who-knows-what. And she obviously doesn't have to give up a year of her life."

"Nicole" Jessie admonished. "Just stop it. At least we have some answers now." She turned to face the attorney and spoke warily.

"Mr. Justice, I get the feeling there is something more that you're not telling us."

Nicole wondered what Jessie meant but remained silent as both women waited for an answer. The attorney moved uncomfortably in his chair and Jessie knew she was right. But a knot had formed in the pit of her stomach and she suddenly regretted pushing the attorney for more information.

"I believe I've given you all the information you came for and" he glanced at his watch "I must hurry over to the courthouse."

As Nicole and Jessie left his office, Nicole turned to Jessie. "What do you think he wasn't telling us?"

"I'm not sure" Jessie said as they reached the car "but I have a feeling all will be revealed somewhere in those little white envelopes."

"Do you think we're ready to open one when we get home?" Nicole asked.

"Let's stop for lunch and we'll decide later. I don't know if I'm ready to face anymore unknowns today."

As they ate lunch, the sisters rehashed the information Mr. Justice had given them.

"Mother was quite the secretive type," Nicole said as she tapped her glass of lemonade. "But how is it that she was married to Garrett and you never even laid eyes on him?"

Jessie shrugged, ignoring her sister's insinuation. "In 2006 I was pretty involved with the ranch and I didn't get to visit mother very often. Mr. Justice said Garrett died in 2007. And now that I recall," Jessie slowly nodded "mother took quite an extended trip toward the end of that year."

"Do you think that was after he died?" Nicole asked.

"I'm betting it was," Jessie agreed. "But you know" she said, "I think we've done enough uncovering for the day. Why don't we lighten up for now and go shopping. You can show me where a personal shopper would find some bargains here in Charleston."

"Well you know" Nicole's spirits lifted at the thought of shopping "I noticed a lovely little boutique on the way over."

The following day, Nicole popped her head into the kitchen and found Jessie reading some of the letters they had found in the attic. Jessie looked up and her eyes – usually sparkling with a smile – were now moist from tears.

"What's the matter?" Nicole slipped into a chair next to her sister.

"Did you know" Jessie sniffled as she spoke "that mother and Garrett had not only known each other, but were in love from the first day they met?"

Nicole nodded but wasn't certain where Jessie was going with it, so she let her continue at her own pace.

"And did you know that dad had cheated on mom?"

"Oh I don't believe that" Nicole said, knowing that neither Jessie nor their mother would have made up such a lie.

"It's here. In the letters mom and Garrett had written to each other."

"Daddy was a cad?" Nicole snatched the letter. "When did this happen? And who was this other woman?"

"Apparently it was a woman he met through business the year I graduated from high school. It doesn't sound like it was a serious thing, but still…" Jessie's voice trailed off as she remembered the photo of her graduation day.

"Let me see if I have this right. Mother met a man that she fell in love with but stayed faithful to daddy, and daddy met a little hottie and couldn't manage to keep it in his pants. Is that about right?" Nicole said.

Jessie faced her sister. "I have to apologize to you."

Nicole was puzzled by Jessie's tone. "For what?"

"That photo on your graduation day? I thought mother was so upset because you were leaving for London. I believed that she was distraught over you leaving for so many years and I never forgave you for doing that to her. But now I realize she found out about daddy's affair on that morning." Jessie's eyes filled as she took her sister's hand. "Can you forgive me for blaming you all of these years?"

Nicole slipped her arm around Jessie's shoulder and tugged her sister toward her. "So" she said lightly "I can shed all of this guilt I've been carrying around? God" she sighed "what a relief."

The next day neither of the sisters seemed anxious to talk about the discoveries they'd made in their mother's letters – least of all their father's affair. But it turned up later that afternoon, like an unwanted relative. The sisters were having their lunch and Jessie started the conversation.

"I'm not sure," Jessie said "But I think mother eventually

managed to forgive him."

"Forgive him, my ass" Nicole sniffed. "I'd never forgive a man who stepped out on me."

Jessie glanced at her sister and laughed. "Maybe that's why neither one of us have a husband. Maybe we're not tolerant enough."

"Letting a man get away with what daddy did isn't being tolerant. That's just...."

"Careful" Jessie warned. "This is our mother you're talking about."

"Yes" Nicole agreed. "The same mother who is expecting us to live together for a year like happy little children."

"Like I said" Jessie sipped her coffee. "Tolerance. Probably one of the lessons mother wanted to teach us but couldn't quite put it in a way she thought we'd accept."

"Yes" Nicole agreed, "because 'Gee your father found some little tart to fool around with, but I forgive him' wouldn't have gone over too well."

As they changed for dinner later, Nicole came into Jessie's room. "I need some new slacks. I think the dry cleaner shrunk this pair. Why don't we get out of the house for a few hours and go to the mall."

"Sure" Jessie agreed, "but before we do anything why don't we see what mother's first 'opportunity' will be. Maybe she'll actually instruct us to go on a shopping spree."

Nicole laughed, "Somehow, I don't think shopping is one of the life lessons mother failed to teach us. We're both pretty good at that task."

"Probably not" Jessie said as she retrieved the small white envelope with Number 2 written on it, "but we can hope," she said as she began to read.

To My Beautiful Daughters,

Each of you has been blessed with the beauty of the Mitchell side of the family. Thank goodness for that because I've known some family trees that didn't bloom quite so nicely. Your physical beauty should never be taken for granted. As you know, I worked quite diligently for my fitness and I believe it is time for you girls to do the same.

I'm certain you can find a suitable outlet and begin to enjoy the rewards of being physically fit.

Love to you always,

"So" Jessie said as she inhaled. "I assume mother wants us to take better care of ourselves?"

"Sounds like work to me" Nicole answered distastefully.

"Me, too" Jessie turned to face her sister. "Why do you think this is the first 'opportunity' she gave us? It doesn't seem so awful."

"Probably to get us prepared for that Survival Camp she's got in one of those letters," Nicole said as she stepped onto the balcony. She suddenly leaned forward, studying something on the beach below them.

"What are those people doing down on the beach?" Nicole leaned closer to the railing.

"Oh them," Jessie smirked. "They come here every week to do Tai Chi on the beach. I guess the sound of the water helps them to concentrate."

"They're fat and they're wearing thongs. Those kinds of people give thongs a bad name." Nicole motioned to her sister without moving her eyes from the beach. "Hand me those binoculars over there will you?"

"Nicole," Jessie whispered. "They're going to see you and

think we're some kind of weirdos."

Nicole looked at her sister and then handed her the binoculars. "You're joking. I'm not the one down on the beach, in a thong I might add, with thighs that look like they survived this century's biggest hail storm."

Jessie took the glasses from her sister and peered through the binoculars at the group of people stretching in perfect unison close to the water's edge.

"Gross," she said. "Did you see that lady with the tattoo on her ass?"

"No" Nicole answered. "What kind of tattoo?"

"I think it used to be a butterfly, but now it kind of stretched out a bit and looks like a really big tree with a head and two wings."

"Yuk," Nicole wrinkled her nose. "I bet she got it when she was in prison for wearing that damn thong in public."

The two sisters laughed and continued to watch the group of people till they finished and started walking to their cars.

"Where are they going now?" Nicole asked.

"Oh, I hear that they go for ice cream at Rick's when they leave" Jessie stated.

"They eat ice cream in thongs?" Nicole continued to watch the group drive down the road like a slow moving funeral procession. "Isn't there some kind of law in this country about sitting in public places with your naked butt cheeks hanging out?"

Jessie laughed at the look on her sister's face. "Thank you for that visual. I will never be able to eat ice cream at Rick's again."

"Just as well" Nicole said as she slid into her chair. "Eating ice cream at Rick's is probably not what mom had in mind for our first opportunity, as she so eloquently put it" Nicole scuffed. "I think she wanted us to learn to take better care of ourselves, eat healthier, exercise... blah, blah, blah."

"I suppose you're right" Jessie replied then eyed her sister. "I think she knew we would lose our edge."

"If it ended in O, we probably ate it" Nicole said as she sipped her drink.

"No" Jessie replied, "I mean I think we need to follow mother's advice and join a gym."

"Why?" Nicole reached for another cigarette and looked curiously at her sister. "Why would we want to do all that sweating and jumping shit, when we could just have surgery? Suck that stuff out, package it up and ship it to some medical research lab."

"You are a cynical bitch, aren't you Nicole? I think what mom had in mind was to actually enjoy the process of working out together, as sisters."

Nicole took a long drag off her cigarette, looking nonplussed at the thought. "We get plenty of exercise. We go shopping - that's walking. And just yesterday Higgins got away from me on the beach and I had to run to catch him. That's exercise."

"He has legs the size of a pretzel, Nicole, how far could he run?"

Nicole remained unconvinced.

"Alright" Jessie conceded "If you won't do it for yourself, just look at your dog. None of his little pink shirts fit anymore." They glanced over at Higgins and Gus, who were snoring contentedly in their lambs' wool beds. "They've had so many Cheetos in the past 2 weeks that we're going to have to buy them bigger beds."

"So sign the dogs up for the gym" Nicole answered, still unimpressed with her sister's idea.

Jessie let the conversation drop for the time, but as they were dressing for dinner later that evening, Nicole popped her head into Jessie's room. Her linen slacks were unzipped and her silk top was pulled tight across her chest. "Okay" she said, "here's another outfit your dry cleaner shrunk. Either he has to go back to dry cleaning school, or you're right. We need to join a gym next month."

"Not next month," Jessie insisted. "We'll look for one first thing in the morning."

"Can we look for a co-ed gym? We could hook up with some guys while we're working out," Nicole laughed.

"Are you crazy? I don't want any man to see me wearing spandex with this spare tire I have around my waist."

CHAPTER 5
I THINK MY INNER GODDESS WENT UNDERGROUND

The following morning, after a hearty breakfast of croissants and maple flavored breakfast sausage, the sisters studied the phone book listings of Spas and Gyms.

"Well," Nicole announced "we've narrowed it down to 5 places." She was now totally committed to losing the extra weight that continued to pile onto her ever-expanding waistline. "Let's do a drive-by. Whoever has the biggest women going inside seems like the obvious choice, doesn't it?"

"Won't that mean they're not losing any weight?"

"No," Nicole stated. "That means we will look fabulous next to them."

"Good point. Let's go."

They climbed into Jessie's car and headed to their first stop. It seemed none of the women going into the spa had eaten anything on the O diet for quite a few years. The second stop was worse. None of those women had eaten food ending in any letter of the alphabet for quite some time. The third stop, Harry's Muscle Shop, looked a bit on the seedy side. Hips and Lips Spa and Surgical Center seemed promising with lots of hefty women pushing their way through the front doors. But on closer inspection of the women coming out, their lips puffed up like marshmallows, Nicole and Jessie decided against their fourth selection.

That left only the Flab to Fab Exercise Spa and the women stopped at the far end of the parking lot to scrutinize the clientele. They studied their unsuspecting subjects, making comments about the height, weight, and girth of each.

"This looks good" Nicole said. "Let's come back after lunch."

Jessie slid the car into gear, ignoring Nicole's attempt to put off the inevitable, and headed to a spot closest to the door. "We'll just go in and have a look around. If we don't like it, we'll go back to the phone book."

They were greeted by Heather, a waif-like receptionist who looked like a slight breeze could pick her up and blow her in to the next county.

"We'd like some information about your gym" Nicole offered.

"Oh, we're not a gym," Heather gushed, her voice as wispy as her waistline. "We're an Exercise Salon, specializing in weight management classes."

"Oh, I understand now. You're a designer gym," Nicole snapped.

Undaunted by the remark, Heather handed Jessie a sheet of paper, "Let me give you the outline of our classes." Heather seemed like a nice enough young lady, and her energetic demeanor and size 4 body only made Nicole and Jessie more determined to shed their excess baggage. They took the list as the willowy debutante led them toward the observation area.

"You mean people can come in here and watch us exercise?" Jessie whispered in horror at the thought of her thighs bouncing like Jell-O as onlookers jeered at them through the glass like peeping toms. Nicole and Jessie watched intently as a dozen rotund women stepped on and off little platforms to the beat of Barry Manilow crooning "Copacabana". Nicole stepped quickly away from the window.

"Jessie," she pleaded, "I don't want to sweat like those women."

"Nicole," her sister countered, "I don't want to *look* like those women. We have to do something." They thanked Heather and quickly headed to the car.

Safely back on the porch with peach martinis, they studied the list of classes.

"The 30-Minute Lunch Time Sweat Shop is definitely out of the running," Nicole sniffed. "Sweating makes my hair frizz up and I'll look like a troll doll wearing spandex."

"What about the Bun and Butt Aerobics? That sounds like fun."

"That sounds like more sweat," Nicole sniffed again.

"Here it is!" Jessie said excitedly. "Dancing with Veils – doesn't that sounds exotic?"

"Yes" Nicole exclaimed, suddenly envisioning themselves in a class they could both enjoy. "Veils are just like scarves, just a bit shorter. I just bought two new Hermes scarves. You can use one. It will look fabulous with your hair color."

A fitness class laced with some fashion, Jessie thought. They had finally hit on a class that would make Nicole happy. "I think this is a good place to start. Let's go shopping for some new exercise outfits."

Mid-morning the following day found Jessie and Nicole tentatively signing on for a six-month stint at Flab to Fab Exercise Spa. Perky Heather tried her best to persuade them into the 2-year plan, but commitment wasn't a strong point for either woman. They'd hoped for a one-month contract, but found six months was the best they could negotiate.

As they left the changing room with their new color coordinated spandex clinging to their bodies and designer scarves tucked securely around their waists, Nicole turned to her sister.

"I can't believe you talked me into this."

"Nicole," Jessie said, "do you remember the thong people on the beach?"

"Okay" Nicole agreed. "But if my hair starts to frizz up like a ball of cheap yarn, I'm just warning you."

A tall, slender woman who smiled warmly greeted them. "I'm Jasmine, your instructor for Dancing with Veils."

Nicole held up the end of the printed fabric that hung loosely around her neck. "We have our new scarves already."

"Oh" Jasmine said, "We have special veils that we use for our belly dancing class."

The sisters tried to hide their surprise. "Belly dancing?" Nicole glared at Jessie. "I didn't realize..." and let her voice trail off.

Jasmine led the women to a dark room that smelled of exotic incense and was draped in dark purple curtains. She stood at the front of the room as Nicole and Jessie slinked to the farthest corner. They quickly surveyed the rest of the women as Jasmine began to speak. "Good morning, ladies. My name is Jasmine and in the next few weeks, I am going to help you find your inner goddess."

"I'd rather she help us find the exit" Nicole whispered.

After 20 minutes of belly rolls, shimmy's and hip gyrations, Nicole and Jessie wondered if the exercise spa had a refund policy. After 40 minutes of twirling veils and snapping their finger cymbals, they knew their inner goddesses were deep in hiding.

On the way back to the house, the women tried to collect their thoughts. "You know," Jessie offered "maybe we should have just rented one of those exercise videos and done this privately."

"Yeah," Nicole said, "then we could pause it whenever we need a break. God, my abs are killing me. I feel like I've been in a prizefight and I'm down on the mat with the ref standing over me counting to ten. I need a nap."

"Did you see some of those women? It looked like a revival of the Aqua-Net queens," Jessie laughed.

"And is everyone in that place named after a damn flower? Jasmine, Heather and I bet they have a Daisy and a Rose tucked away in the back. Are we going back or do you want to retire our special veils?" Nicole teased.

"I think we should go home and practice, so that we look like we know what we're doing next time. And we'll get some

Aqua-Net for that frizzy hair of yours," Jessie teased.

"Okay," Nicole laughed, "but if my inner goddess doesn't show up soon, I want a refund."

After their third session of gyrations, hip motions, and finger cymbal lessons, the girls returned to the house with renewed allegiance to their plan.

"Mom would be proud," Nicole stated as they greeted the late afternoon sun the way they greeted the sun every afternoon – with a peach martini. "We haven't had any foods from the O diet in over a month" Nicole continued. "I know that I've lost seven pounds."

"How do you know that?" Jessie said turning to her sister. "We promised not to weigh ourselves until we finished all of our classes."

"Screw that!" Nicole said as she lit another cigarette. "I'm not dancing around with those freaking veils for the fun of it. I want to wear a cute little bikini and look like those stick girls named after flowers down at the gym."

"OK," Jessie conceded. "I think we should treat ourselves and go to Atera's"

"What kind of food do they serve?" Nicole asked.

"Atera's isn't a restaurant, honey," Jessie said as she refilled their martini glasses. "It's a swimsuit boutique named after the Greek Goddess of water. I promise you'll love it."

"The last time you told me I'd love something I ended up dancing with veils in a purple room that smelled of incense with 6 other goddess- searching freaks."

The next morning after a breakfast of strawberry crepes without the whipped cream, the girls drove to Atera's swimsuit boutique. "Have you shopped here before?" Nicole asked her sister.

"Once 3 years ago when I was about 2 sizes larger then I am now." Jesse pulled her car into a parking space. "The sales girl asked if I was shopping for my daughter, so I left and went to Wal-mart. They don't ask any questions at Wal-mart."

As they stepped through the Greek columns that surrounded the entrance, a tall brunette wearing a white veil that covered her from head to toe greeted them. A gold belt with tiny coins that made a small jingle when she moved was wrapped around her waist.

Nicole whispered to Jessie, "If these sales girls are named after flowers, I'm leaving."

The sales girl with the tinkling gold coins around her waist greeted them in a wispy voice, "Hello, my name is Athena. Can I set up a dressing room for you ladies today?"

"That would be great," Jesse said. Athena glided across the floor in her white scarf. "Could I interest you in some wine or tea while you shop today?"

"Got any martinis?" Nicole asked.

"She's just kidding" Jessie said to the sales girl as she eyed her sister. "White wine would be fine."

The boutique was decorated with life size sculptures of Greek gods. White gauze fabric was draped from the ceilings and a three-tier water fountain flowed soothingly in the center of the store. "This place might not be so bad," Nicole said as she turned to Jessie, "serving wine in the dressing room. You think they do that so we'll convince ourselves we've found our inner goddesses while trying on swimsuits?"

"No" Jesse smiled as she flicked at a price tag hanging from a silvery suit. "I think they do that because they charge $400 for a swimsuit."

Athena helped the girls make a few selections and placed them in their dressing rooms. To their horror they discovered there were no mirrors in the dressing rooms so they were forced to model each swimsuit in the spacious – and thankfully private –

outer room. When Jessie saw her sister trying on a yellow polka dotted thong bikini she knew she would need more than one glass of wine.

Twenty-five swimsuits, three glasses of wine and several hours later, the girls had made their choices. Nicole had settled on a black bikini with 3 silver coins just below her navel, a very tropical printed one piece, but had thankfully resisted the polka-dotted thong bikini. Jessie had picked out a white bikini with tiny blue flowers and a solid black one piece.

As they carried their purchases into the house, Jessie turned to Nicole. "You know," she started, "since we started this whole physical fitness thing, I really do feel better."

Nicole smiled, "You feel better because we just spent a thousand bucks on swimsuits that make our inner goddesses shine in our size 6 bodies."

They decided to treat themselves to a quiet dinner at a trendy restaurant called "The Shady Lady". As they shared a bottle of wine and salads, Nicole spoke softly. "I guess you're right," she stated.

"About what?" Jessie asked.

"About feeling better. Sometimes I think of mother and realize that she must have been terribly disappointed with us."

Jessie smiled at her sister. "I've thought of that too. Maybe we can make it up to her now. You know, by doing the things she wants us to do in her letters."

Nicole sighed. "I hope so."

As the evening wound down and the girls deposited themselves back on the porch, they talked about it again. "I'm very happy to be back down to size 6, and" Jessie smiled at her sister, "I think mom would be happy for us, too."

Nicole nodded, "This physical fitness idea that mother pushed us into wasn't awful. Do you think she knew we'd let ourselves go after she was gone?"

Jessie pondered the idea for a moment. "I suppose so. Mom was pretty perceptive about us. She saw things about each of us that we didn't see in ourselves."

They sat quietly for a few moments then Nicole quickly jumped to her feet. "It's time," she announced. "The next letter....we have to open the next letter."

"Fine" Jessie agreed reluctantly. "But let's wait until tomorrow. I'm exhausted." She looked curiously at her sister. "What do you think she has in store for us this month?"

"I don't know" Nicole laughed, "but I hope it involves a man. I'll bet a good looking chap with a tight butt could help me find my inner goddess."

CHAPTER 6
LET THE GAMES BEGIN

Stepping out onto the porch the next morning Jessie stopped to watch her sister who was lying in the lounge chair in her new black bikini. Tan and toned with her red curls draped across the back of the chair, Jessie thought she looked like a movie star. Stretched out next to her Gus and Higgins slept together wearing their new dog visors and sunglasses that Nicole had bought for them the previous day. She told Jessie that they needed to protect their eyes from the UV rays and all dogs should get a new summer wardrobe to impress the other dogs on the beach. Jessie gave in; she had learned over the past few months to pick her battles with her sister.

"Well aren't you three a pretty sight," Jessie said as she poured herself some coffee. "You were right, Nicole; our little guys are looking pretty sporty today."

"I told you they would love their little visors. Look how happy they are," Nicole beamed. "I think we should buy them some of those surfing shorts with the little Hawaiian flowers on them today. Don't you think they'd look cute? Higgins likes pink but I think Gus would look good in yellow, being black and all. But I guess he would look good in anything."

"Can I ask you something?" Jessie picked up Nicole's juice glass. "Did you mix champagne with your orange juice again today?"

"It's one of the things I love about living on the beach," she laughed. "Everyone here is on vacation and today so am I."

"I thought we were going to open another letter today," Jessie said pulling the letter from her pocket.

"I already know what's in it, dreamed about it last night. That's why I'm pretending I'm on vacation." Nicole took another sip of her drink. "And before you read it, you might want to fix yourself a drink too."

"It was in my room, how did you read it?" Jessie waved the letter in the air. "Why you little pickpocket, you snuck into my room while I was sleeping."

"I didn't have to. I'm psychic. I just know what it says; I don't have to read it." Nicole said as she poured herself another drink. "It starts out with 'My darling little offspring, I am the most controlling dead mother you will ever meet, but I have lots of money and in order to get it you have to perform tricks for me. I want to be entertained even while I'm dead. So for this month's entertainment I would like you to cook for the orphans, give away all your earthly belongings and chant with the Tibetan monks. Does that sound about right?" Nicole asked as she poured her sister a drink.

"Except for the monk thing" Jessie laughed. "I don't think

she liked the chanting monks with their brown robes."

"Black robe, brown robe, I really don't see the difference," Nicole answered. "Either way, they could both use some new clothes. They've been wearing the same thing for like a million years now. Remind me to send them my resume."

"That's a good idea," Jessie answered. "Just look what you've done for our dogs. I'm sure they'll hire you."

"Monks would look cute in visors and sunglass," Nicole laughed. "It would go with that whole bead thing they have going on." Jessie grabbed Nicole's drink and slowly poured it over the balcony.

"I think it's a little early for so much champagne, don't you agree?" she asked.

"Wow!" a voice from across the balcony said. "You must have been a real party animal at those college frat parties."

"Thank you, Andre," Nicole answered as she poured herself another drink. "Would you like some?"

"Got my own," he gestured holding up his glass. "Ben is out of town for the day and I had to find something to do to pass the time."

"So Andre," Nicole shouted. "Jessie and I were just about

to read another one of mom's letters. You want to join us?"

"Nicole," Jessie whispered, "It's none of his business what mom had to say." But before she could continue she heard Andre coming up the stairs. He sat in the chair next to Nicole and turned to Jessie.

"Let the games begin!" Andre said as he refilled Nicole's glass. It was one thing to constantly be dodging Nicole's remarks and keeping her in check had become a full time job for Jessie, but now with Andre egging her on there was no telling what could happen. It was like trying to lasso a great white shark with a strand of yarn.

"Andre," Nicole turned in her seat, "Remember I told you how mean mother was treating us in those letters?"

"It's her revenge," Andre stated. "You planted her in a cold, white marble urn between her two husbands. Did you think you wouldn't have to pay for that one?"

Jessie turned to face Andre. "Our mother is not in some tangent universe planning revenge. She simply wanted to insure that Nicole and I grew closer and that we gain enough experience to lead healthy fulfilling lives."

"Yes," Nicole muttered. "I now know how to color coordinate bowling balls in my garden. That's a life lesson I couldn't have lived without."

"I think you're being a bit dramatic, Nicole. We've only opened one letter and it wasn't even terrible. We had to take an exercise class. That wasn't so awful."

"Oh yes" Nicole turned to Andre and giggled. "Belly dancing lessons. That will get me farther in life than my university education, for sure."

"Well we will never learn any more about what mother has in store for us until we read this," Jessie said as she opened the envelope and slumped back in her chair. Her eyes scanned the page and she began to read aloud.

To my dear daughters,

I have long believed that pride and humility are opposing forces in life only when pride becomes arrogance and humility turns to pity. Privileges in life should never be construed as entitlement and this, my darlings, may be your most difficult lesson.

You may find this hard to believe, but there are people in your very community that need you. They don't need your money, they don't need your food, and they certainly don't need your pity. They need the one thing you can give them and never take back.

They need your time.

I'll leave you to ponder this with an open mind and a loving heart.

Love,

Mother

"No shit," Andre said. "You weren't kidding about your mother being mean. Now she wants you to work with people who won't work for themselves?"

"So you see what I was talking about?" Nicole said to him. "She's got a whole pack of these surprises in store for us. She packaged them up in little white envelopes and plans on torturing us each month with a little twist in our lives."

"You're both so sarcastic I can't stand it," Jessie piped in. "There are plenty of people who are having a very difficult life and just need some help to get through a tough time."

"Oh puh-lease," Andre rolled his eyes. "Are you going to bake cookies and distribute them downtown?" He poked his finger at Nicole's arm and laughed. "You girls are a couple of trust-fund babies who think a rough day is not being able to get an appointment at the spa. What do you know about volunteer work?"

"Look," Jessie said, "there are places we can call and find out about volunteering. Besides" she picked up the letter and scanned it "are we sure that's what mother meant?"

Andre rose to leave. "As much fun as this has been, I'll leave the two of you to figure it out. I'm sure," he flicked the corner of the letter with his finger, "your mother will lead you toward enlightenment."

The girls sat in silence for a few uncomfortable moments, neither one wanting to break through the wall of ice that seemed to have suddenly appeared. Nicole picked up the letter and read it to herself. Once finished she took her cigarette lighter and lit the corner of the paper, tossing it into the ashtray. Sliding from her seat she turned and walked into the beach house.

"Where are you going?" Jessie asked.

"To pack" Nicole replied.

"Just like that? You're giving up our inheritance?" Jessie said.

"No, just mine." Nicole spun to face her sister. "I've done a lot of things in these past few months all in the pursuit of our precious inheritance. I've danced in dark smelly rooms in search of my inner goddess. I left my job and my friends in London to come live here. And I admit that I am very thankful to have gotten to know you. But why in God's name couldn't she just leave us the money and let us go on with our lives?"

"I think she felt guilty," Jessie said in a whisper.

"Guilty? For what? Why would anyone feel guilty about leaving their daughters eight million dollars?" Nicole asked.

"I think she knew she was going to die young and wouldn't have time to teach us the things that moms teach their kids," Jessie answered.

"With $4 million dollars I could hire someone to teach me some life lessons" Nicole answered. "Besides, shouldn't she have thought of that before we hit our thirties?"

"Apparently that was not her point" Jessie stated.

"As I see it, her point was to provide herself with a full year of entertainment from her heavenly quarters," Nicole scoffed.

"Pretty expensive side show don't you think?" Jessie laughed. "Look, I'll make a deal with you; I will find the easiest form of volunteer work that is out there. Something that's suits your personality, if you promise not to go back to London."

Nicole pondered this for a few moments. "OK, I'll stay" she said. "But if I end up dead because you have me volunteering in some homeless shelter, mom's year of lessons will seem like child's play when I'm done haunting you and that pinhead lawyer."

After scanning the local papers and phone books the girls had narrowed it down to delivering meals on wheels to the elderly or working in the local thrift shop.

"I'm not sure if I want to go house to house delivering meals," Jessie said. "And honestly, I don't think I want food spilling all over my car. So I guess if you're leaving this decision up to me, I think we should volunteer at the thrift shop."

"What exactly is a thrift shop?" Nicole asked. Jessie eyed her sister and decided to soften the blow. "It's like a small specialized boutique."

"For some reason I don't think you're being completely honest with me," Nicole said. "I know exactly what you're going to say: it'll be fun, it'll be an adventure Nicole, and really how awful can it be to work in a boutique for a few hours a week?"

The following week, after several outfit modifications, Nicole had settled on simple black slacks, sandals and a silk violet top. Jessie had tried to convince her sister that today was more about comfort than style, but she might as well have been speaking a foreign language.

Driving through the cobblestone streets in the older

section of the city, Jessie watched as her sister twirled her hair around her finger, a habit Nicole had since she was a little girl.

"Who would put a boutique in this section of town?" Nicole asked as she checked the locks on the car.

"It's a thrift shop," Jessie answered.

"I think your exact words were SPECIALIZED BOUTIQUE when you talked me into this," Nicole quipped. "What exactly is their specialty, sweatshirts and camouflage pants? And who the hell shops in this part of town?" she said, not bothering to cover her distaste.

Jessie pulled the car in front of the store and a scruffy looking character appeared at Nicole's window asking for change. Startled, Nicole tried to shoo him away like a fly that had landed on her toast. The man wandered off, chatting happily to himself and ignoring the two women as they stepped from the car. Jessie heard someone call her name and turned to find Willie Jones smiling as he walked toward her.

"What in the world are you doing in this neighborhood?" he asked as he approached.

"Willie," Jessie smiled. "It's nice to see you. Do you remember my sister Nicole?"

"Well I'll be," Willie smiled. "Miss Nicole, are you here for a visit? I haven't seen you since you were just a young girl."

"Yes" Nicole said. "Just a visit."

"We've come to do some volunteer work," Jessie offered to Willie.

"Volunteer work? Well good for you" the old man grinned. "Good for both of you. Why, your Mama would be so proud of you she'd be calling all over town to brag on the two of you."

Jessie and Nicole laughed and Willie excused himself to go visit his best girl, he said, Miss Violet. Willie had been on Pawley's Island as long as Jessie could remember. He knew everyone and was one of their family's friends that had helped their grandmother and then their mother with anything that needed help around the house. He was a wise old character that was known and loved by everyone on the island. The girls waved goodbye and promised to call him soon, then turned their attention back to the thrift shop.

The front window of the store hadn't been cleaned since the Carter administration and was crammed with stuffed animals, old hats, and children's toys from the 1960s. Nicole slid a tissue over the door handle and pushed her way inside. Looking around, Jessie and Nicole weren't certain what they should fear more - the man on the street or the inside of the store. A tall athletic girl in her twenties sat behind the counter talking on a cell phone. When she noticed Jessie and Nicole, she stashed the phone in her purse.

"Hello ladies," she said as she stepped over a pile of cloths strewn across the floor. "Welcome to the Treasure Chest. Is there something in particular you ladies are searching for today? I just had a whole box of designer hats dropped off yesterday."

"Oh no, no, no," Nicole said as she waved a finger at the young girl. "We're not here to shop, young lady. We would never. . ."

Jessie cut her off. "Hi, I'm Jessie and this is my sister Nicole. You must be Jenna," she continued. "Peggy down at the agency sent us here to help out for a few weeks. She tells us that you're leaving to go do some volunteer work in Africa."

"Yes, I'm so excited," Jenna said, almost bouncing with enthusiasm. "A group of us will be building a new school for the orphans, so I'm not sure how long I'll be gone. Are you girls on probation or some kind of work release program?" she asked.

"A work release program from our crazy ass dead mother," Nicole answered without missing a beat.

Undaunted by Nicole's remark, Jenna continued. "I didn't think Peggy was ever going to find anyone to work here," she gushed as she reached for Nicole's hand. "I was really starting to get worried."

"Go figure," Nicole said wearily. "I don't know why there's not a line down the street crawling with applicants. Can you tell us exactly what it that we will be doing here?"

"Oh, it's really easy and a lot of fun" the young girl offered. "You see some really interesting things come through those doors. I can't believe people throw some of this stuff away."

"I can't believe people bought it in the first place," Nicole murmured. Nicole glanced over at Jessie who was rummaging through a cardboard box overflowing with used dog toys. "That is exactly how my sister described it, fun and easy."

The young girl continued, undisturbed by Nicole's obvious distaste. "The door on the right is for drop offs. People are allowed to drop off between 9 and 5. Then we take the items to the back and sort through them and display them around the store."

"And why do we display these things?" Nicole asked as she picked up a torn scarf and then dropped it back into the box. "So people can buy them, of course!" Jenna stated, oblivious to Nicole's growing disgust.

"What kind of people buy this stuff?" Nicole said as she held up a baseball cap from a 1979 Rolling Stones concert.

Ignoring Nicole, Jenna continued. "Let me show you around" she said as she headed for a room filled with books.

After the girls had the complete tour of the Treasure Chest, they learned how the register worked and were given a set of keys. Jenna left and told them to call Peggy if they had any other questions. Within minutes of her departure their first customer arrived staying only a few minutes and leaving without any type of purchase.

"This place is a shit hole," Nicole remarked as she ran her hand across the dusty counter and blew the dust into the air. "No wonder no one wants to buy anything. We probably couldn't give this crap away. In London I shopped for some of the wealthiest woman in the city and now look what I'm doing. I wish mom were alive so I could give her a piece of my mind."

"You know, Jessie," Nicole ranted, "if I would have known what she had in mind for us after she died, I wouldn't have dressed her so nice for her viewing. I would have dressed her in this shit. How do you think she would have felt wearing a tee shirt with a faded blue smurf on it, holding a cabbage patch doll in that coffin? How do you think she would feel when all her friends came to pay their respects? What if someone I know comes in here and sees me? Did she think about that when she forced us to work like child laborers? NO!"

"Are you done?" Jessie was once again tiring of her sister acting out like a two year old. "First of all, you are from another country, no one knows you here. Second, do you really think that Charles or Camilla are going to fly over on a private plane and somehow find their way to Pawley's Island and then say 'Oh yeah, I heard about this really cute boutique; call the limo. Let's go shopping.' What planet are you from anyway, Nicole?"

"Fuck you, Jessie."

"Where are you going now?" Jessie asked as Nicole headed for the door. "Go ahead and run back to your petty little life in London; I'm tired of fighting with you today."

Ignoring her sister's remark Nicole stormed out the door and within minutes returned with the man who had been asking for change. "This is Carl" Nicole said to Jessie. "He's accepted a job with us for a few days."

Jessie raised her eyebrows, and motioned for Nicole to come to the back room. "You hired this guy? Have you lost your mind?" Jessie was pacing and peeking through the curtain to where he stood. She half expected to see the man stashing goods under his shirt and making a beeline for the door, but Carl was just standing where they had left him.

"Isn't this what we're supposed to do?" Nicole asked innocently. "We're supposed to help people. Well," she pointed toward the shop "I'm helping him."

"Oh my God," Jessie threw her arms up. "You don't know anything about him. He could be a drug addict or a rapist."

"Oh stop it," Nicole scoffed. "He's a carpenter. He lost his job about a year ago and has been doing day labor. His kids moved back with his mother and he sends her whatever money he can."

Jessie looked at her sister and shook her heard. "How do you know all this?"

"I interviewed him out on the street," Nicole answered, as though Jessie should have been able to figure that one out.

"You interviewed him?" Jessie said incredulously. "And you fell for this story?"

Nicole peeked through the curtain, then swung it open and said "Carl, can you come here for a moment?"

"Yes ma'am" he said as he walked toward the sisters. "Carl" Nicole said assuredly "how many children did you say you had?"

"Two, ma'am. A boy and a girl." He fumbled in his pocket and drew out a tattered leather billfold. "I have their pictures right here." Jessie and Nicole leaned closer as he took two dog-eared photos from his wallet.

"This was last year, so they'd grown a bit when I saw them last month." The sisters looked at the faces that stared back at them. The kids seemed to be about 10 or so, with blond hair and smiling blue eyes.

"Twins" Carl said proudly. "Smart as can be, too."

"What are their names?" Jessie was touched by the innocence in their faces.

"Joey and Jessica" he answered.

"Jessica" she repeated softly. "That's my name."

Carl looked at her and offered a kind smile. "Yes, ma'am. Your sister told me that. She called you Jessie."

"Yes" she smiled back. "People call me Jessie."

"Little one always wants to be called Jessica. Tells people that's her name. Not Jess or Jessie. My name is Jessica. That's what she tells people."

"Well" Jessie said warmly "she sounds like a girl who has a mind of her own."

"That she does," Carl answered and Jessie saw both the pride and the sadness in his face. She understood why Nicole had instantly trusted this man.

"So," Nicole clapped her hands "should we get started? I told Carl we could pay him $300 dollars a week but he'd have to work for every penny of it."

"Hard work doesn't bother me, ma'am," Carl answered.

"I'm happy to take care of things for you."

"Okay," Jessie gently tapped Carl on his shoulder "but you have to lose the ma'am thing. It's Jessie and Nicole, if you don't mind."

"Yes, ma'am," Carl laughed. "I'll have to get used to that, though."

"By the way" Jessie called after him "what is your wife's name?"

Carl stopped and a new sadness came into his eyes. "Her name was Bethany. She died two years ago. Cancer."

"Oh." Jessie and Nicole glanced at each other. "I'm so sorry."

Carl nodded. "I am too" was his only answer as he shoved his hands into his pockets. "Where would you like me to start?" he asked after a moment. "I could build some shelves for some of these things."

Nicole instructed Carl to remove everything blocking the front window and take down the dingy curtains. She suddenly looked like she had done this all her life. Within hours the windows had been cleaned, floors had been swept and signs had been hung in the front window. CLOSED FOR REMODELING. The girls worked for days stopping only to eat or sleep. The walls had been painted a deep violet, racks of cloths were organized into dresses, blouses and pants, and dressing rooms with full length mirrors had been constructed in the back of the store. Books that once had been scattered around the store in cardboard boxes were now organized alphabetically on bookshelves. Carl had set the mismatched china on tables with linens; tablecloths and wine goblets and furniture had been positioned around the store to give it a more inviting atmosphere. Tables had been placed in the back to organize the incoming donations and by the end of the week the store was unrecognizable from its previous life. Jessie, Nicole and Carl seemed pleased with what they had accomplished. On Saturday the store reopened for business and within minutes was filled with customers.

"Is this still the Thrift Shop?" Jessie overheard a lady ask Nicole.

"Why yes it is" she heard her sister say. She watched as Nicole escorted the lady to a rack of clothes and picked out several outfits with coordinating hats and scarves. Later Nicole rang up the woman's purchases and placed them neatly into a purple bag that she tied up with matching ribbons. The bags had been Nicole's idea and she had paid for them out of her own pocket, telling Jessie that people would pay more if their purchases were wrapped up in cute little designer bags with ribbons. It seemed to be working.

Carl was in the back packing up the second set of dishes

he had sold that day. A week ago he had been begging for change and now look at him, Jessie thought. Nicole had showed him how to dress and set him up a cot in the back of the store telling Jessie it was for security reasons. Jessie knew better. Nicole wanted to protect him like a little brother. In a few weeks the girls would be leaving the thrift shop and Carl had agreed to take over the vacant position. The sisters were paying him out of their own pockets, and agreed to continue to do so until Carl could get back on his own feet.

A few days later over martinis on the deck, Jessie was going over the books for the thrift shop. "This has been the best week yet since we started working there" she remarked to Nicole.

"I'm not surprised," she answered as she poured another martini for herself and Jessie.

"What do mean?" Jessie asked. "It's all about presentation. When we walked in that place it looked like some teenage gangsters had ransacked it. No wonder they couldn't sell anything. We took the same stuff and presented it well and poof," Nicole gestured with her cigarette. "We can't get it on the shelves fast enough. And that idea you had about renting the truck and picking the furniture up at people's houses?" she paused. "That was pure genius."

"Thank you," Jessie smiled. "I thought so too. I think I'm

going to miss working there."

"Well I have to admit that I enjoyed making that place over, but tomorrow I am going to show you my idea of a specialized boutique. And we are not coming home until your car is overflowing with cute little designer shopping bags," Nicole laughed.

"Hey Nicole," Jessie smiled at her sister. "I just want to say I'm really glad you're here. It's been fun having a sister these last few months. Maybe mom knew what she was doing with those letters after all."

"Maybe you're right," Nicole said as she stretched her back. "But tomorrow it's my turn to teach you something" she said as she pointed to her sister. "I am going to teach you how to shop with the big girls."

"Fine" Jessie answered "but tonight we're going to open door number 4 and find out what mother has in store for us next." Jessie opened the envelope and began to read aloud.

My Darlings,

Your Aunt Gert has had a bit of a rough time since she ran off her last husband Walter. Be patient with her. My sister is one of the most unique individuals I have ever known. While mother and father didn't always approve of her eccentricities, they understood that Gert simply marched to a different drummer. She can be trying and funny and caustic, but she was my best friend.

Continue to bring Aunt Gert the gift of being good listeners.

Eternal Love,

Mother

"That's it?" Nicole said as she took the letter from Jessie. "I can't believe that all we have to do is go visit our curious Aunt Gert every few weeks, listen to her ramble on about her ex-husbands and we'll be that much closer to $8 million dollars. Hell, I could do this with my eyes closed," Nicole grinned. "Hey," Nicole's eyes held a hint of hopeful mischief. "Let's open the rest of the letters."

"We can't do that!" Jessie was stunned at the suggestion.

"Why not?" Nicole said. "Do you think Mr. Justice is going to channel some message through a psychic and tell mom that we opened all the letters at once?" Nicole asked.

Jessie rose from the table and turned to her sister. "I want to open the letters in the order that mom wrote them. It was her last wish, Nicole. The least we can do is grant her that much. Now if you will excuse me, I am going to bed. We'll call Aunt Gert in the morning," she said as she turned and walked into the house.

"Alright," Nicole pouted. "We'll do it your way." Nicole said as she followed her sister inside. "But I still think Aunt Gert is nutty as a fruitcake. If she wants us to take her shopping for bowling balls, I'm going to start looking into a nice nursing home," she laughed.

CHAPTER 7

AN ELEPHANT IN A COCKTAIL DRESS

The girls spent the next few days packing and making arrangements with Aunt Gert for their visit.   The morning they were to leave Nicole came down the stairs in a panic, followed by Higgins who was wearing a matching pink nightshirt and doggie slippers.

"We can't go!" she shouted.

"What do you mean we can't go?" Jessie said as she tried to calm her now hysterical sister.

"Higgins and I were watching the weather channel and there is a hurricane headed right for Charleston," Nicole screeched. "I heard them say it was a category 10...or 20 or something."

Jessie started to laugh and Gus came to her side to investigate. "First of all Nicole, I know in England a hurricane is a rare occurrence, but this happens all the time on the coast and I know that Charleston hasn't had a hurricane come across in at least 10 years. It will probably blow right past us," Jessie said, still trying to settle her sister's obvious panic.

It took Jessie an hour to reassure Nicole that they were not going to be carried away by the hurricane or end up living in a makeshift shelter with 50,000 people eating cold beans from a can, waiting for the National Guard to rescue them.

Finally they were on their way to Charleston, Higgins and Gus huddled together in the back seat like they had been best friends all their lives. Hopefully, Jessie thought, she and Nicole could learn to do the same.

A few hours later they were driving down Daisy Lane in Charleston. "Oh my God!" Nicole said as she yanked the sunglasses from her face. "I forgot about the bowling ball garden. We have really got to talk to her about planting some flowers." Nicole eyed her sister. "What do the neighbors say about having bowling balls in her yard as her shrubs?"

Jessie glanced around the yard and smiled. "Aunt Gert really doesn't care."

Just then Aunt Gert emerged from the front door carrying her small white dog. To Jessie's horror, the dog was wearing a huge jeweled collar and Gert had on a huge flowered dress that flowed around her like an ocean of daisies. "Welcome back" she called with a long southern drawl that always reminded Jessie of their mother. "Toto got all dolled up for your visit."

"Aunt Gert," Jessie greeted as she opened the back door to free the now very active dogs. "How have you been?"

"I didn't get a chance to finish telling you girls why I ran off that old geezer Walter," Aunt Gert said as though she were picking up a conversation that was already in progress. "He thought I was fooling around with every man in town. Can you believe that?" She was a bundle of energy packed tightly into a tiny frame. "A woman my age sleeping around. Hell, I didn't even want to sleep with him. He snored like a damn freight train. Men... who needs them. Anyway" she paused long enough to hug each of the women. "I'm glad you girls decided to come for a visit but there's a hurricane headed our way. Looks like it's going to come right through our pretty little town."

"Is it now? " Nicole said as she glared at her sister. "I'm sure it will blow right past us. These things always fall apart when they hit land," she paused then added "or so I've been told."

"Come inside. I fixed you girls some lunch and we'll talk about some hurricane preparations," Gert said. She deposited the little white dog inside the door, who was followed immediately by Higgins and Gus, tails wagging and noses to the ground following their newfound friend.

After a lunch of crab cakes and lobster bisque the girls headed to the store with a list of hurricane supplies that Gert had given them. The first item on the list was sandbags. They would need these, Gert had explained, to ward off the rising waters from the storm. At the sand distribution center the girls were shocked when they were given a small shovel, a stack of empty plastic bags and directed to a pile of sand. Nicole hesitated for a moment then reached into her purse and pulled out a fifty-dollar bill and offered it to the attendant. "We're going to get a latte, we'll be back in an hour" Nicole said as she held out the shovel and the bags. "Fill as many bags as this will buy and please load them into our car if you would, but try not to get any sand on the seats."

"Ma'am," the attendant grinned, "that's not quite how it works. You'll have to load up your bags quickly and then move along so the other folks can get their sandbags."

Nicole grabbed the fifty from the young man and stormed back to the car. "Do we have a Plan B?" she said to Jessie who was enjoying the entire scene. "I am not," Nicole continued indignantly "going to stand here shoveling sand in this heat." She paused and then looked at her sister. "Is this what you pay taxes for? For the pleasure of digging like someone on a chain gang?"

Jessie tried to stifle a laugh by clearing her throat. "I can't load up all of those sand bags by myself, so I suggest you come up with a better idea."

Ten minutes later the girls were walking into the garden department at Wal-Mart. Jessie and Nicole had decided on a dozen 20 lb bags of top soil and took their place in line with dozens of folks who seemed to be unnerved by the staggering media blitz warning of the impending disaster.

As the girls stood in line, they surveyed the other shoppers and the contents of their carts, which seemed even more peculiar than their own. The woman in front seemed to be purchasing enough cereal to feed a third world country and the gentleman to the rear was obviously going to light that third world country with every flashlight and battery the store had to offer.

"Gonna do some gardening?" the clerk asked.

"No," Nicole answered as she shot Jessie a dagger. "I'm using the dirt to bury my sister after I kill her tonight."

"Really, Nicole," Jessie insisted, "this storm is going to blow right past us."

"Then let's stop and get a Martini and watch it go by from the bar," Nicole offered.

Just as the bartender placed two martinis down for the girls, Jessie's cell phone rang. It was Gert and she sounded as huffy as the storm.

"It's a category 4 and 200 miles away from Charleston," she advised Jessie. "Where are you girls?" she asked sternly.

Jessie assured her they would be right home as she watched her sister guzzle the remainder of her drink.

Once back at Gert's the rest of the day was spent hauling plants, lawn chairs and other would-be projectiles out of harm's way. Watching Nicole unload 240 pounds of topsoil to ward off the floods of evil rain, she realized what a trooper her sister was beneath the cosmopolitan facade.

Later that evening, as the rest of Charleston was glued to the weather channel, Gert and the girls settled in to watch a movie. Before the first bowl of popcorn had been consumed, the lights had begun to flicker and the sound of the howling wind surrounded them.

The hurricane had arrived with all the subtlety of an elephant in a cocktail dress.

With total disregard for hurricane safety, the three women huddled together in front of the kitchen window to watch the action outside. The three dogs, on the other hand, were safely snuggled together in the hallway.

Tree branches flew past the windows and the sliding doors bowed ominously from the wind. Suddenly Jessie had an idea.

"I've never stood in a hurricane before. When the eye passes over us, let's go outside."

Nicole gave Jessie a look as though she had just sprouted horns from the side of her head. "I don't think that's in the Hurricane Safety Manual."

"Neither is sitting in front of a glass window with hundred mile an hour winds howling on the other side of it. Besides," Jessie called over her shoulder "if you won't go with me, I'll just go out there myself."

"Oh we'll both go," Nicole huffed. "Because if you are picked up by the wind and end up living in a tiki hut in Bora Bora, it will be fun spending your share of the inheritance."

Armed with a flashlight the size of a fountain pen, the girls inched their way along the front wall of the house as Gert watched anxiously from the safety of her perch at the kitchen window.

"Are you sure we should be doing this?" Nicole shouted to be heard over the wind. "I really do want to live long enough to spend all that money we are going to inherit."

Fully expecting to be the only storm chasers in the neighborhood of retired folks, the girls were shocked when they saw half a dozen spotlights flickering through the treetops like mutant fireflies. It took only one powerful gust to send them scrambling back to the perceived safety of the kitchen window.

For the next 90 minutes they watched as the storm ripped hundred year old oaks from the ground and dumped them onto the neighbors' cars and houses. Power poles tumbled like dominoes and anything that had been left outside was now a flying weapon.

"Is this what you people from South Carolina call blowing past us?" Nicole asked as she lit a cigarette. "And don't even think about telling me I can't smoke in here," she glared at Jessie.

Gert emerged from the kitchen carrying a pitcher with three martini glasses. "This is how we people from South Carolina deal with Mother Nature, Miss Nicole," she said pouring the girls each a drink.

After two pitchers of martinis, the girls were both giddy and numb. "So Gert," Jessie pried, "Why did you finally run Walter off? He seemed like a really nice man." "Well" she began as she grabbed Nicole's pack of cigarettes. Nicole shook her head as she now watched Gert attempt to light a cigarette. "I woke up one night," Gert began. "It was 3:00 in the morning and I heard Walter outside yelling and carrying on and making a terrible racket. I ran outside and there he was," she stood and added the physical effects to her story "waving a gun, screaming at the imaginary men to go away and stop looking in the windows."

"So I take it there were no men outside looking in the windows?" Nicole said as she lit the cigarette dangling from Gert's lips. "So who was he yelling at?" Jessie asked, not sure if she was more amused by Aunt Gert's story or her attempt to smoke a cigarette.

"Not who...what," Gert barked. "Fireflies! The fireflies were out that night and the old geezer thought there were men hiding in the trees smoking cigarettes and peeking into my bedroom window. So the next morning I kicked his sorry butt out."

"Well at least he made it out alive," Nicole said as she glanced at the mantle where 2 urns were placed neatly side by side. The three women chuckled and poured another drink.

"Dick and Harry."

"Are you kidding me?" Jessie laughed as she touched the plaques on the bottom of the urns. "Your deceased husbands' names were Dick and Harry?"

"Not exactly" Gert said. "That's just what I call them, and what the hell do they care, they're all dead."

Nicole raised her glass and in a voice fuzzy with peach martinis said "Gert, honey, you southern women are OK."

The next morning Nicole and Jessie were awakened by the buzz of chain saws and the hum of generators. A group of neighbors stood outside the window drinking their coffee. An elderly man still wearing his bathrobe tapped on the window. "Your girls OK in there?" he asked.

Nicole and Jessie pulled the sheet up to their necks and answered. "Yes, we're OK."

"How about some coffee?" the man in the robe asked. "Hank down the street is making coffee on his gas grill and later he's going to fry up some eggs and potatoes. Would you girls like to join us?"

"Sure we'll be right out" Jessie answered.

"I can't believe we're lying in bed talking to a man who is still in his robe about frying eggs and grilling coffee," Nicole whispered to Jessie. "Beam me up, Scotty." Just then the pack of three dogs bound into the room and onto the bed. "I guess we need to take the kids for a walk," Jessie laughed.

"I'm going to take a hot shower and then we'll take them out," Nicole said as she pulled the curtains across the window.

"Not gonna be any hot shower this morning," Jessie's warned.

"We lost electricity, not water," Nicole said impatiently, knowing there was an explanation on the way that she didn't think she wanted to hear.

"The pump that runs the water heater is electric," Jessie's said.

"I sweated all night without air-conditioning and now I can't even take a shower?" Nicole crawled back into bed.

"Let's take the dogs for a walk and check out the damage," Jessie said as she pulled the covers away from Nicole.

The girls opened the front door and stood silently on the front porch. The road was barely visible. Massive oaks lay across neighbors' houses and cars. Tree limbs, power lines and shingles covered the ground. The once beautiful community now looked like a war zone. Gert's house had survived with minimal damage, only the shutters had been ripped from the windows. Gus, Higgins and Toto seemed puzzled at the disappearance of a once beautiful lawn.

The man in the robe walked over and handed the girls each a cup of coffee. "Gert OK?" he asked.

"She hasn't woke up yet," Jessie replied. "We stayed up a little late last night," she added as she looked at her sister.

"Is anyone hurt?" Nicole asked.

"Not that we've heard," he replied.

The sisters and the dogs walked the neighborhood for almost an hour. Street signs were bent and gnarled and trees lay on the ground twisted and broken. Everywhere they walked people called out asking if they were OK. The girls had never met any of these people, yet their concern seemed genuine and heartwarming.

They headed back to the house and worked for hours to

clear enough debris to get the car out of the driveway. Exhausted, filthy and smelly, they dragged themselves into the house. Gert had fixed a lunch of crackers and cheese and lukewarm tea, but it tasted as good as any food from a five-star restaurant.

For the next three days the girls worked side-by-side to help Gert clean the yard and house. The entire neighborhood would meet every evening at Hank's house where they would cook food from their now-warming freezers on his gas grill. Bottles of wine were passed around and poured into plastic cups. People told stories of previous hurricanes, and they all agreed that this had been bad but not the worst.

Nicole and Jessie had tried for days to talk Gert into returning to Pawley's Island with them, but she would have no part of it.

"This is my home and these are my friends. This is where I want to be," she explained as she walked with them to their car. Gert thanked them for all their help and they agreed to stay in touch and visit again soon.

As they pulled out of the driveway Gert came running from the house with a paper bag. "What's this?" Jessie asked.

"It's a surprise. Don't open it till you get home," she instructed and blew kisses to both of them.

Once home they surveyed the minimal damage and retreated to the porch with a pitcher of martinis to watch the setting sun and talk about how lucky they were that the hurricane missed the island.

"Wow!" Jessie said as she turned to Nicole. "These are the best martinis you've ever made."

"That's what was in the bag that Gert gave us." Nicole gave Jessie the hand written recipe for Gert's Famous Peach Martinis.

"So you think mom would be proud of us?" Nicole asked softly. "I think right now she is smiling down on us and yes, I do think she would be proud of us," Jessie answered in a whisper.

"Well that's all good. But tomorrow mom's money is paying for a long massage and a manicure," Nicole said as she held out her nails for Jessie to see.

"Hey Nicole, you know what time it is?" Jessie asked.

"Yeah, its time to go to bed," she replied.

"No its time to open the next letter," Jessie said simply.

"Like I said," Nicole laughed, "its time to go to bed."

"Are you afraid mom's next challenge will keep you awake?" Jessie teased.

"No," Nicole smiled as she took the envelope from Jessie and opened it. "I'm afraid she's going to send us to work on a farm or make us volunteer to work at the local prison to help rehabilitate the dregs of society."

Nicole opened the letter and began to scan the page and began to read.

Nicole and Jessica,

I remember many years ago, as a young girl, I was out sailing with a friend and his family when an unexpected storm blew up. We were many miles from the shoreline and it took a great deal of effort on everyone's part to get us to safety. The father of the young man I was with was calmly directing each of us on what our job was so that he could lead all of us to safety.

I learned a valuable lesson that day. If any one of us had not worked together, all of us could have been lost.

You will eventually have many opportunities to work together and I trust you will do it with unselfishness and love.

Put this lesson to the test when you can, and you will find it to be a valuable reminder that none of us walk alone.

Love,

Mother

Nicole and Jessie looked at each other questioningly. "Isn't that what we just did? Work together to clean up that hurricane? You know the one," Nicole said. "The one that blew right past us?"

"Okay, so I was wrong about it. And yes, we did just work together. So I wonder what she wants us to do," Jessie said.

"I told you," Nicole answered. "She wants us to work together with criminals."

Jessie chuckled at her sister's sarcasm. "I didn't hear anything in that letter about the prison system," she said as she continued, "and I think mother was involved with animals, not prisoners."

"Oh," Nicole said. "Do you think she wants us to go clean the animal cages? Ugh...what a disgusting thought."

Jessie rolled her eyes. "I think," she said as she got up, "that mother just wants us to learn about teamwork, but I'm not sure how or where that will be."

Jessie paused and turned to Nicole. "And I'm not sure," she said as she wrinkled her forehead "if mother intended us to actually enjoy the process of learning teamwork."

"You're right" Nicole agreed laughing. "I think suffering through each of these life lessons is more in line with her thinking."

"I don't know if she wanted us to suffer" Jessie added "but I do think she wanted us to be serious about her assignments."

"I'm not sure how serious I can be while I'm searching for my inner goddess one week and fighting a hurricane another week. No," Nicole said, "suffering was definitely what mother had in mind."

CHAPTER 8
I WANT TO BE A COWBOY

The phone rang early Thursday morning and Jessie picked it up with her free hand.

"Jess" the deep voice said "its Jake."

"Hey" Jessie said, warming to the sound of the voice she knew she missed. "What's going on? How's everything at the ranch?"

"Good" Jake answered "but I need to ask you about something."

"What's up?" There was no concern in Jake's voice and Jessie assumed it was just the usual call she got from Jake every few days.

"I got a call this morning from the Jacobson ranch."

"Harry Jacobson? What did he need?" Jessie liked Harry Jacobson and respected the old rancher's treatment of both animals and people.

"Seems there was a raid on a place down in Florida and they came up with about a dozen horses that are in pretty bad shape. Harry can only take 5 and wanted to know if we could manage the rest of them."

Jessie sighed as she always did when someone came to her with animals that had been abused or neglected. "How bad are they, Jake?" she asked.

"From what I hear, they're pretty thin. They haven't been fed or exercised much in quite some time. Been locked in some kind of a pen." The disgust in Jake's voice was apparent, but Jess wasn't prepared for the next piece of information.

"They had to put 3 of them down, Jess." Tears welled in her eyes and Jessie stayed silent for a moment, then Jake continued. "I'm sorry to put this on you first thing in the morning, but I wanted to make sure it was okay with you to take the other 4."

"Of course, Jake. Call Harry back and make the arrangements. Call me back and let me know the timeframe." Jessie placed the phone on the cradle and looked at her plate of fruit, then wrapped it and placed it in the fridge. She no longer had an appetite. Her shoulders were slumped and her eyes were red as Nicole swept into the kitchen.

"What's up?" Nicole asked. "You look a bit down this morning." Nicole reached for a cup from the shelf and poured herself some hot coffee. "A bit early in the day to be so glum" she said as she leaned against the counter.

"Problems at the ranch," Jessie answered but offered no more. Nicole glanced at her sister.

"Can't that good-looking manager handle the crisis?" She smiled and sipped her coffee. Jessie leveled her gaze softly at her sister and smiled back.

"Jake can handle just about anything," she said as she walked to the ringing phone.

"Yes..." she listened intently. "Okay, sure, that's fine. I'll be there before they arrive." She listened as Jake spoke, then interrupted him "Jake, I know you can handle it but you know I want to be there for this type of thing." Again, Jake spoke at his end of the line and Jessie glanced at her sister, then rolled her eyes as Jake continued.

"Jake....JAKE" she said to get his attention. "I'll be there tomorrow, sometime around noon."

As Jessie and Jake spoke, Nicole grew more curious. What's this crisis, she wondered. Why is Jessie going back to the ranch? And, she thought suddenly, how long will she be gone? Her thoughts were quite tangled by the time Jessie hung up the phone.

"So," Nicole said, "you're going to go off to the ranch for a couple of weeks and let me stay here in this blistering heat to fry like an egg?"

Jessie gave her sister a puzzled look but said nothing. "And" Nicole continued "do you honestly think Mr. Justice won't find out and be forced to give all of our money to some dogs and cats so they can screw their pedigree brains out in luxury?"

Jessie smiled, still looking quizzically at Nicole, but quickly began to see Nicole's tirade as just the morning entertainment she needed to take her mind off the call from Jake. When Nicole finally began to wear herself down, Jessie smiled at her sister.

"Nicole," she conceded, "you're totally right."

"I am?" Nicole narrowed her eyes and looked suspiciously at her sister. "You never think I'm right."

Jessie laughed and went to stand by her sister's side. "That's absolutely not true, Nicole. I remember one other time..." Nicole jabbed her sister playfully in the ribs.

"So what...are you going to let me come to the ranch with you?"

"Of course" Jessie replied then added "and we won't even have to sneak out. I'll call Mr. Justice and explain the situation. If he says it will be a breach of the will, then neither of us will go. However," Jessie said devilishly "when I tell him I think this is the perfect opportunity for our teamwork assignment, I don't think he'll have a problem with it."

They drove through the quiet morning mist, the hazy humidity still hanging in the air when they arrived at Jessie's ranch. The sign over the entrance welcomed them to "Peace of Paradise" and Jessie smiled as she took in the familiar sights and sounds of her beloved ranch.

"So you'll take care of the sick horses here?" Nicole asked as she looked across the field where several horses grazed.

"Yes," Jessie said warmly. "We'll take care of the ones that are coming today. But remember I told you that we also take care of horses that can't race anymore but are still young and vibrant." She looked over at Nicole and smiled. "Injured horses certainly take more care and more time, but when they get back on their feet, it's like they know they've been given a second chance. They're grateful."

Nicole and Jessie locked eyes and each felt the unfamiliar warmth of sisterhood pass between them. Jessie pulled her car to the front of the house and turned to her sister.

"How is it," she smiled "that I turned to animals and you turned to people?"

Nicole paused then laughed. "I'm not sure. Environment, I suppose." They shrugged and went into the house, where the smell of fresh flowers greeted them.

"Oh" Nicole stopped and studied the expanse of the open rooms. "After Pawley's, this place looks even more magnificent." The wood floors were polished and glistened in the mid-day sun that spilled through the windows. Tall vases of fresh flowers sat on a table in the center of the foyer and another in the corner. Nicole walked silently to the large living room where a stone fireplace went up two stories, revealing dark wood beams that gave the room a welcoming sense of openness.

"Well, I don't know about magnificent" Jessie chuckled "but it's home and I love it here." She paused then added, "I didn't realize how much I missed it until just now."

The second floor of the house looked down over the living room and fireplace. The hallways were fitted with thick beige carpet, and the walls were painted a warm cocoa. Each doorway led to a generous bedroom with a private bath, and each was decorated more beautifully than the other.

"Jessie, this place is wonderful. How could you ever stand to leave it for a year?"

"Well, I confess," Jessie smiled "I wouldn't have left here had it not been for the idea of getting to know you."

Nicole laughed, "Yeah, sure. Getting to know me and what eight million dollars feels like."

"Okay" Jessie said as she linked her arm into her sister's "now let's go find Jake."

It didn't take them long since Jake was standing in the hallway as they entered. Jessie's breath caught slightly at the sight of him, tall and lean, cowboy hat in hand, and arms that were firm from hard work.

"Hey," he smiled at the sisters. "I saw the cloud of dust as you came up the drive. Thought I'd take a break and say welcome back."

Jessie went to Jake and gave him a quick hug "Thanks, Jake" she smiled. "What time will the horses get here?"

"Couple of hours" he replied. "I've got the barn ready whenever you want to take a look. And Doc Warner is coming by first thing in the morning to check them over." He glanced at Jessie as he continued "Won't be pretty, from what I hear."

Jessie shook her head. "I just don't understand people."

"Well" Nicole offered "at least there are places like this and people like you to take care of them now."

Jake and Jessie nodded at Nicole, and then Jake spoke again. "Miss Nell said she'd come by and fix some lunch, but I sure could use a cold drink."

Nicole noticed once more how easily Jake fit into the house, and wondered again if there was more to her sister's feelings for Jake than Jessie was willing to admit. She decided then and there that they were the perfect couple, and if Jessie wasn't willing to admit it, then Nicole would just have to play a bit of cupid.

"Jake" she asked innocently as they walked to the kitchen "how long have you worked here?"

He smiled as he spoke, "Ever since I moved here from Colorado - close to 6 years now."

"Really?" Nicole answered. "And you two have never"

"Nicole!" Jessie interrupted. "Jake and I are friends."

"Besides" Jake smiled, "it wouldn't be a good idea to get

too 'friendly' with the boss lady."

"Oh, I don't know," Nicole said, "it seems like you two know each other so well, and you just make the cutest couple."

Jake raised his eyebrows and laughed, and Jessie's mouth dropped in horror at her sister's obvious suggestion. "I just think you should start to look at each other in a different light," Nicole continued, unfazed by the reaction her comments were having on Jake and Jessie.

"Do you now," Jake said, encouraging Nicole to continue. "And just what 'light' do you think we should"

"Don't champion her cause, Jake," Jessie interrupted. "She gets her kicks out of embarrassing me."

"Maybe," Jake's eyes locked with Jessie's "I think her cause has some merit."

Nicole felt the electricity between Jake and Jessie and smiled as she congratulated herself. Mission not accomplished, she thought, but it's definitely on its way.

Jessie looked away and went to the fridge to get some lemonade. Desperate to change the subject, Jessie said, "How bad are they?"

Jake gave Nicole a quick wink and a wicked smile before

Jessie could turn back around. Nicole smiled triumphantly, then sat at the table and looked out the window as she listened to Jake and Jessie talk about the horses and the business of running the ranch.

After lunch, the three of them climbed into the golf cart and rode the short distance from the house to the barn. They teased Nicole about how inappropriate her wardrobe was for the ranch and Jessie said she would loan her sister some jeans and boots. The barn was expansive and clean, but Nicole turned her nose up at the distinct smell of horse, hay and alfalfa that permeated that air.

"Do I have to shovel anything while I'm here?" Nicole asked impatiently. Jessie laughed and kicked at the stray pieces of hay that lay about.

"I don't know," she teased. "We'll have to see how you behave."

By the time Jessie entered the barn at 7 the next morning, Doc Warner, their friend and local vet, was already checking the second horse. "Hey Jess" he greeted her warmly but his face was serious.

"Doc" she nodded to him, and walked toward Jake to leave the vet while he studied the horses. She smiled as she greeted him.

"Good morning."

"Hey, Jess" he smiled warmly, and gave her a comforting squeeze around the shoulder. "Doc says it's not great, but it could be a whole lot worse. Mostly they're undernourished, haven't gotten the best of care, no exercise...typical crap that people do."

"Well," Jessie smiled, "we know all too well how that goes."

Doc Warner stood and walked toward them, his face grim and set. "I'm pretty sure we have at least one serious problem" he started.

"How so?" Jake asked.

"Could be West Nile on the chestnut." Jessie and Jake glanced sadly at each other, knowing what the outcome would be if the old vet was correct in his diagnosis.

"What do you suggest?" Jessie asked.

"Let's keep a close eye on her the rest of the day, keep her in the stall for now."

Jake nodded toward the horse, which was probably beautiful in her day but now looked confused and thin. "What should we watch for?"

Doc Warner slid his fingers through his thinning hair and looked from Jessie to Jake. "I'm pretty certain that's what it is, but I've been in this business long enough to know nothing is certain. Watch for any change in her behavior, if she seems dizzy or if she seems to lose her balance."

"Could it be something other than West Nile?" Jessie was hoping for some good news, but wasn't surprised when she didn't get any. The vet shook his head slowly. "Probably not, Jess. I'm sorry."

"What about the others?"

"Surprisingly," he answered more cheerfully "they don't look too bad. Need some meat on their bones, and need to work back into an exercise routine, but I have confidence you and your staff can handle that."

"See you tomorrow?" Jake said as they walked toward the vet's truck.

"Actually," he called as he got into his truck, "I'll stop back later this afternoon."

Jake and Jessie walked back to the barn. "I'm sorry, Jess," he said. "I know how upsetting this is for you."

She nodded but no words would come through the thickness in her throat.

"I'll have Sam take care of some things in here," he motioned around the barn "so he can keep a close eye on her." Jake patted the pretty chestnut colored horse on her back. "I'll put Cooper and Brian in charge of the other new ones."

Jessie nodded and looked up to see Nicole walking toward them. "Wow," Jessie remarked, "it's not even noon."

"Very funny," Nicole said. "What are you two doing out here?"

Jessie explained to Nicole what Doc Warner had told them, giving a brief explanation of West Nile Virus in horses. Nicole walked toward the stall where the horse stood. "So there's no cure?"

"Not at this stage" Jake offered.

Nicole nodded, sadness filling her eyes. She stood silently, stroking the horse's head and neck. She spoke softly to the mare "I'm so sorry, Brownie," she said. "I think I would have liked you." She looked questioningly toward Jake. "She seems fine."

"I know" he said "but she's not. She'll start to suffer in a few more days."

A small sound escaped Jessie's throat, and Jake walked back to her side. "Why don't you and Nicole go back to the house."

She nodded and looked into his eyes. "I think we will for a while. Thanks, Jake."

"Hey, cowboy," Nicole called back to Jake. "Join us for breakfast?"

"Thanks," he called as he waved. "Already ate. Maybe tomorrow."

When Jessie and Nicole returned to the barn in the late afternoon, the beautiful chestnut colored horse was gone. Jessie didn't ask but she knew Doc Warner had taken her to be put down. It saddened Jessie but she knew that at this point there was little else to be done.

The next morning, as promised, Jake was at the house by 7 for breakfast. Miss Nell fixed a solid breakfast for all of them, then quietly disappeared.

"As long as you're here" Jake said as he stabbed at a pile of pancakes "I might as well put you two to work."

Nicole's face paled and she placed her fork back on the side of her plate. She cleared her throat and said "Work? I thought I was just here as a token observer."

Jake smiled his most appealing grin and said "Everyone at

the ranch works at one point or another, don't they Jess?"

Jessie nodded and said "Everybody. It's true, Nicole. You know," she smiled "it's that teamwork thing mother told us about in her last letter."

Realizing that neither of them were having a laugh on her, Nicole began to fidget like a child. "What is it you'll have me do then?"

Jake and Jessie exchanged a quick glance. "Well," Jake started nonchalantly "Brian, Cooper, and Sam are pretty tied up with the rehab for the 3 new horses we took, so some of their chores are getting behind."

"Chores?" Nicole gulped and looked at her sister. "What kind of chores?" She had visions of being knee-high in horse manure.

"For one thing," Jessie said to Jake "I noticed the feed is getting low. It needs to be re-stocked"

"That's one," Jake nodded. "But Kat and Sadie haven't had a good bath since yesterday."

"BATH?" Nicole shrieked. "You want me to bathe a horse?"

Jake and Jessie looked wide-eyed at Nicole's reaction. "Nicole," Jessie said impatiently "we haven't asked you to saddle-train them. Just wash them down."

"I ride them," she sniffed. "I don't bathe them."

Jessie took her plate to the sink and said, "You do now."

After a quick lesson on how to wash down the horses, Jessie and Jake stood back until they were sure Nicole could handle the task she'd been given. As they walked toward the back of the barn, Jake and Jessie laughed quietly as they heard Nicole muttering while she worked. Jake or Jessie checked in on her every so often and she seemed to be handling the chore fine. She was covered in soap and bits of hay were stuck to her boots and clothes, but Nicole seemed determined to show that she could take care of cleaning a horse.

"Good job," Jake called as he saw Nicole walking Sadie back to her stall. "All done?"

"Well I sure as hell hope so," Nicole said as she spit a piece of hay from her lips. "What will you have me do now, master? Shovel the horse poop?"

"Needs to be done, if you're volunteering," Jake laughed.

"Oh I don't think so," she said. "Besides" she handed the reins of the horse to Jake, "I don't think I could lift my arms." Jake laughed and walked the gentle horse back to her stall.

"Look," he called after Nicole, "Sadie wants to say thank you for making her feel better." Nicole walked toward the horse who nuzzled her shoulder as Nicole patted her head. "You're welcome, Miss Sadie," she said. "And thank you for bathing with dignity, not like that other bruiser." She nuzzled the horse again and began to laugh at the tickling sensation. "That Kat critter almost flattened me he was so fidgety."

Jake laughed as he watched the exchange between the horse and Nicole, then led Sadie back to her stall.

"Why do you have to bathe them?" Nicole asked Jake as they left the barn.

"Because they can't bathe themselves," Jake answered. "They can't do anything for themselves. These animals - like all domestic animals - depend on us for their food, their health, their exercise. We've taken them out of the wild, and now it's up to us to see that they have the best life we can give them."

Nicole nodded and let Jake continue. "It's why I admire your sister so much. She gets it." He stopped and nodded toward the field where Jessie was working with one of the newly adopted horses. Nicole stood beside him and watched as her sister gently tugged at the animal, urging it to take a few more steps, then a few more.

"She gets it?" Nicole asked. "You mean she gets how to take care of horses?"

Jake smiled but didn't move his eyes from Jessie, watching her work the horse, building its confidence and trust in her. "Jessie gets it all," he said. "She sees the line between helping them and letting them keep their independence."

They stood quietly for a long while, watching until Jessie handed the horse off to one of the ranch hands and walked toward where they stood.

"You're amazing," Nicole said in awe. "The way you talked to that horse. I swear it understood every word you were saying."

Jessie patted the dust from her jeans and smiled. "You think I can talk to a horse? Jake here can read their minds," she laughed. "Now that's something to see."

As they walked back to the house, Nicole was again taken by the easy exchange between Jake and Jessie. She resolved that this could be her own little mission: get her sister hooked up with someone who was obviously the man of her dreams.

Even if Jessie was too stubborn to admit it.

The next few weeks were filled with chores and errands. Nicole had become quite the helper and volunteered for almost any task that needed to be done. She watched as Jake and the ranch hands tended to the heavier work and she helped her sister with areas that required less expertise. Nicole thought of the recent letter their mother had left for them, and realized they'd gotten the opportunity to work as a team much sooner than either of them had imagined. She smiled as she leaned the pitchfork against the wall of the barn.

"I didn't realize you enjoyed pitching hay so much," Jessie commented.

"Trust me," Nicole said. "It's not the hay that has me smiling."

"What then?"

"It's as though mom could see what this past month would be for us." Nicole took Jessie's arm as they walked from the barn. "Remember? The letter about teamwork?"

Jessie nodded, recalling the letter. "I remember. So what do you think of ranch life?"

Nicole stopped and turned toward her sister. "You aren't going to try and talk me into becoming a ranch hand now, are you?" she laughed.

"With a little more training, you'd be a natural" Jessie laughed. "You should give it some thought."

Nicole nudged her sister's shoulder and smiled. "Got any

more ranch managers like Jake? I might give it some thought if you did."

Jessie laughed as they entered the house, but for the hundredth time that day, her thoughts turned to Jake and she felt a stab of regret that she would be leaving for Pawley's Island in the morning.

"Oh, by the way," Nicole mentioned as they walked. "Jake is taking us to dinner tonight. His treat."

Jessie turned to her sister and started to object, then hesitated. "Fine" she said "but I don't want to hear any comments about Jake and me becoming a couple."

Nicole smiled, shrugged, and walked up the stairs, calling over her shoulder. "Be ready by 7" she waved "and don't wear those jeans." She stopped on the steps and turned to her sister. "Try to look devastating."

Jessie glared up at her sister and said "If Jake wanted someone devastating, he'd be going after you."

"If he were going after me," Nicole said, "I wouldn't be as hard to catch as you are."

Jessie fumed. "I am not running away from him."

"Oh? And what would you call it?"

Unable to come up with a suitable response, Jessie just shook her head and walked to her room.

Hmmm, Nicole thought, this might be harder than I thought. Jessie is so stubborn. She smiled to herself and muttered "Cupid may need a bigger arrow."

Jake arrived just before 7 and found Nicole sitting in the living room, looking lovely. She rose as Jake entered the room and gave him a quick hug.

"Listen, Jake," she started, "Jessie is being quite stubborn about my whole match-making plan."

Jake held up his hand. "Nicole," he started "I appreciate your....effort to get Jessie and I together, but if she's interested in pursuing anything other than what we have, I think it should be Jessie's decision."

"Oh my God," Nicole said. "You obviously know nothing about women."

Jake laughed as Nicole continued. "Jessie is crazy about you. She's afraid that if things didn't work out that it would ruin your friendship."

"Wouldn't it?"

Nicole rolled her eyes. "Why do both of you assume that it wouldn't work out? Can't you see how perfect you are for each other?"

Jake rubbed the back of his neck and looked at Nicole. "I don't know," he said skeptically.

"Jake," Nicole said "trust me on this one. Jessie has this inner goddess that is drooling to get at you."

Jake narrowed his eyes at her. "Inner goddess?"

Both turned as they heard Jessie come into the room. She eyed Nicole suspiciously but said nothing.

Jessie wore a yellow sundress that made her copper tan glow and the blue in her eyes look electric. She carried a small, black leather purse that matched her shoes, and her hair hung loosely around her shoulders.

"Wow!" Jake said. "You look pretty fabulous, Jess."

"Thanks," she smiled. "You don't look so bad yourself. And of course," she turned to her sister "you're the one who looks devastating."

Jake had made reservations at The Day's End, a small restaurant that was famous for its fine food, friendly atmosphere, and a jazz quartet that had been playing on weekends for the past few years. Dinner was filled with easy conversation and Jessie was thankful that Nicole restrained herself from any remarks about her and Jake.

After dinner they went to the lounge for a drink, and Jessie was strangely aware of Jake. He seemed to be sitting closer than usual, paying closer attention to her, and sending off a vibe that made Jessie's skin tingle with excitement. As they drove home, Nicole was unusually quiet and when Jake pulled to the front of the house, she hurried from the car claiming a headache.

Jake walked Jessie to the porch and they sat on the swing as they talked.

"It was a lovely evening, Jake. Thank you."

"It isn't often I get to see you outside of the ranch. It was a real pleasure for me." Jake slid his fingers through Jessie's and lifted her hand to his lips. "We should do this more often."

Jessie smiled but said nothing.

"I'll see you tomorrow before you leave?" he asked.

"Yes," she answered. "Why don't you come by for coffee and we can talk about the rescue horses."

They stood and Jake put his arms on Jessie's shoulders as he looked into her eyes. "It's not horses I want to talk about,

Jess."

She stood perfectly still as Jake placed a gentle kiss on her mouth. She smiled and stepped back.

"I know, Jake. But I have some things to think about."

Jake nodded and turned to leave, then stopped and turned back to her. "I'm a patient man, Jess, but even I have my limits."

She nodded. "I know," she said softly and watched as Jake turned and left. Jessie stepped into the hallway, walked to her room and before her head hit the pillow she knew she was in love with Jake.

What she didn't know was what to do about it.

CHAPTER 9
NEW HAIR, NEW MAKE-UP...NEW BOOBS

August on Pawley's Island is 98 degrees by ten in the morning with tourists arriving in droves. Every rented beach house is overflowing with vacationers who come here to relax and get away from the city. These are the ones that don't want the circus-like atmosphere of Myrtle Beach and opt instead for the quiet, unassuming ambiance of this small coastal town. They arrive with enough baggage and knickknacks and oversized SUV's to fill the entire state of South Carolina. Two and three families share a house, all with litters of kids between them.

Willie stopped for a visit and he and the sisters made a sport of watching the families from the deck. Every Saturday they met and had breakfast while placing their bets on the incoming victims.

"I bet $20 that the guy in the black Volvo with the blonde girlfriend will be fighting by this time tomorrow," Nicole said as she placed a $20 bill in the middle of the table.

"You're so cynical. Why would you think that? They look like lovers on a holiday," Jessie said as she set a plate down in front of Nicole.

"Because he's gay," Willie said without lifting his gaze from cooking breakfast. "Oh my God!" Jessie said. "She's turned you into a sneering little creature, too. How did this happen? One day you're this sweet, gentle person and now you're, you're . . ." her words trailed off. "You're just like her."

"Good morning, girlfriends," a voice yelled across the deck. The girls looked to see André standing by the railing in a red satin robe drinking coffee from a Crystal wine glass.

"Morning, André," Willie waved.

"I'm sorry, Willie, I didn't see you standing there behind that big black grilly thing. What are you cooking? It smells marvelous."

"Shrimp and grits," Willie answered as he spooned the southern delicacy onto some plates. "There's plenty if you and Ben want to join us."

"No thanks, I'm trying to watch my figure" Andre laughed as he patted his abs. "Hey, speaking of watching figures, have you seen that beautiful hunk of a man driving the black Volvo yet? Who's he trying to kid? Showing up with that blonde girlfriend. He's about as straight as I am," he said as he whirled across the deck. "Too da loo ladies. I'll see you later for cocktails"

"I don't believe it," Jessie said as she thumped the table. "You have corrupted the whole island. They should name a damn hurricane after you. Hurricane Nicole comes ashore with gale force winds leaving only the most stubborn and corrupt people who will eat their young for survival."

As Willie and the girls finished their breakfast they continued wagering on the rest of the unsuspecting tourists. Everyone watched as a young couple gave their 5 year old a time out for leaving his new electronic game outside on the porch overnight. It rained last night and the game was now sitting on top of the trash covered with last night's spaghetti.

"I remember when I was a kid," Willie said as he lit a cigarette. "My parents would take us on vacation and the only thing we had to play with was paper and crayons. My brother and I would make up games like counting blue and red cars, or how many cities we would drive through. Had to have an imagination, not like kids nowadays. Have you girls seen the kids building sand castles on the beach? They've got buckets and shovels and things that make castle shapes. Hell, all we had was a seashell and an old Dixie cup that would fall apart from pushing it into the sand all day.

"God, are you old," Nicole commented. "I can't believe they even had Dixie cups back then. Are you sure it wasn't the Holy Grail you used?"

"Very funny, Miss Nicole," Willie said as he picked up his things to leave. "I've got to get going. Got a date today with Miss Violet from over in Sweetwater."

"Have fun," the girls said together. As they watched Willie

drive off Jessie went in to the house and returned with a white envelope.

"Guess who we've got a date with?" she said as she opened the letter.

"And just when I thought the day couldn't get any more perfect. Go ahead if you must," Nicole motioned to her sister.

Jessie began to read.

My Darling Daughters,

I trust by now you have gotten to know each other and realize what wonderful women I have always known you both to be.

I was lucky as a child because I grew up in the same house as my sister Gert. What wonderful memories we made along the way. It created a bond between us that was never broken throughout our lives. I knew even in my final days that I could count on my sister for anything. And that, my darlings, is the strongest bond you will ever have with anyone in your entire life.

I loved your father dearly, for many different reasons, but the relationship I had with my sister was even stronger. I hope over the past few months that I have provided you with some opportunities to create trust between you that will last for the rest of your lives.

So this month I would like for the two of you to put that trust to a test. I know that both of you have your own styles that come from growing up on different continents. I've always found it quite intriguing to see the difference in people from various parts of the country and the world. I would like for you to put your trust in each other this month. There are many ways you can do this, but I have selected a mission that should be both fun and enlightening.

I would like you to give each other a makeover. Please let go of your inhibitions and your stale old habits and dare to be different! You may be pleasantly surprised at the results but I do have one rule you must follow: Neither of you has ever looked good as a blonde.

Happy thoughts.

Love

Mother.

Jessie glanced at her sister who had a cynical look on her face. It was the first time that Nicole had not thrown one of her famous rants about their mom's Life Lessons. "So what do you think? Jessie asked.

"Too bad," Nicole answered as she reached across the

table to fluff Jessie's hair. "I think you would have looked great as a blonde".

Jessie leaned back in the chair out of Nicole's reach. "I don't think mom meant us to turn each other into freaks," Jessie said.

"Trust me, sister. That's exactly what she meant. This is going to be fun, don't you think?" Nicole said.

"No, I don't think it's going to be fun," Jessie said as she pulled her hair into a ponytail. "I think it's going to be a really long month. I sure hope mom is enjoying this show from wherever she landed."

"Oh don't get so huffy," Nicole laughed. "When I'm through with your hair and your boobs and your clothes, Jake will be falling all over himself to get to you."

"My boobs?" Jessie said as she crossed her arms in front of her chest. "What the hell is wrong with my boobs?"

"What boobs is more like it." Nicole stood, pushed her chest forward and began to strut like a peacock in heat. "These are boobs, dear," she said. "This is the best money I ever spent. Hell, they cost more than my first car. And they've gotten me a whole lot farther than that freaking car ever did."

"You had a boob job?" Jessie said as she studied her

sister's chest. "I never knew that."

"I was living in another country," Nicole said as she lit a cigarette. "Did you want me to send you a letter or postcard? Hey sis, how's everything, weather's great and oh by the way I'm enclosing a photo of my new tits."

"I'm your sister, I should know things like that," Jessie said feigning hurt feelings. "And don't get it in to your pretty little head that I'm going to get a boob job. Jake likes me just the way I am."

Nicole leaned forward "The key word here is 'like'. When I'm done with you Jake is going to LOVE you. And you don't need to have a boob job, just a little lift and push would help. We really do need to get you out of those training bras."

"And while we're at the mall," Jessie said "we'll stop by the Lancôme' counter and have them show you how NOT to wear so much makeup."

"Oh my God!" Nicole gasped. "That's just mean. I do not wear too much makeup."

"It takes you an hour to put your face on in the morning just so we can walk the dogs." Jessie said. "Who cares if you have makeup on when you're walking on the beach? Hell, little Higgins is even dressed up, for God's sake."

"I care" Nicole pouted. "What if we're walking down the beach and George Clooney or Antonio Bandares comes strolling along. Wouldn't you want to look your best?"

"You aren't serious, are you?" Jessie laughed. "And I suppose you dress Higgins up just in case George or Antonio happens to have their dog with them?" "Exactly," Nicole answered.

"I have never heard of a celebrity sighting on Pawley's Island. I think we should just get dressed and go to the mall."

"So what do you want to do first?" Jessie asked as she pulled the car into the spot. "Makeup or hair?"

"I say we start with your training bra," Nicole remarked. As the girls strolled through the lingerie department, a woman with a measuring tape dangling from her neck and silver glasses teetering on her nose approached the twosome.

"Can I help you ladies today?" she asked in a prim voice.

"I would like to have my sister measured for a new bra," Nicole answered.

The saleswoman turned her attention to Jessie. "And when was the last time you had your measurements taken?" she asked.

Jessie thought the woman reminded her of the nurse in her doctor's office: And when was the last time you had a colonoscopy exam?

"In gym class in 8th grade apparently," Nicole's muttered. The saleswomen led Jessie into the dressing room and Nicole stood outside tapping her foot like an anxious child. Once 36C was the determined number she busied herself picking out bras for her sister to try on.

"You don't really think I'm going to wear that?" Jessie said as her sister handed her a lacy leopard print bra.

"Just try it on. You might surprise your inner goddess who, by the way, is just roaring to get out." Nicole laughed as she pulled it off the hanger and handed it to Jessie. "And try this one on next. It's a water bra. The saleswoman says it's the latest thing in pushup bras."

"Oh great," Jessie laughed. "If I'm ever stranded on a desert island I can drink my bra." Jessie held up the pink bra. "Don't they have just a plain white bra in this store?" she asked.

"If we wanted plain white bras we could have stayed home

and gone shopping in your top drawer," Nicole answered as she pointed Jessie back to the dressing room.

"I'm not sure about this," Jessie said as she looked at herself in the mirror. "I mean sure it looks great now and under cloths but what happens when you take it off in front of a man?"

"You mean in front of Jake," Nicole corrected.

"Well yeah, isn't it like leading them on with a promise of big boobs and then when you're naked, POOF," she waved her arms. "He'll say 'Oh shit what happened to the big boobed girl who was here a minute ago."

"Do you really think that once a guy has you in the sack he really cares whether you have big tits or not? Hell, you could have horns on your ass and a tattoo that says Property of Folsom County Prison. They don't care what your tits look like. They're about to have sex with you and their brains are not the part of their body they're thinking with right then," Nicole answered.

The girls laughed and finally gathered up their choices. Jessie purchased 2 black, one red and 3 lacy bras with push and squeeze capabilities. The water bra and the leopard print were returned to rack.

"Ok," Jessie said as she pulled her sister's arm and led her up to the cosmetic counter. "It's your turn now."

"Shouldn't we eat lunch or something first?" Nicole protested weakly.

"Hey, you had your fun, now it's my turn." Jessie guided Nicole into the seat at the counter.   A young girl wearing a white lab coat came over to greet them. "Hi, ladies, my name is Daisy."

"Oh God, not another one of those freaking flower girls," Nicole whispered to her sister.

"How can I help you today?" Daisy asked.

"I would like you to show my sister how to wear a little less makeup," Jessie said. "I think a more natural, less time consuming routine is what we're looking for."

"All right then, let's get started shall we?" The bubbly little cosmetician said as she began to remove Nicole's makeup. "My, my, we do have some makeup to take off here don't we," she commented as she threw the 4th cotton pad into the trash. "How much time would you like to spend in the morning applying makeup?" Daisy asked.

"None, really. But I guess God wasn't having a feel good kind of day when I came along. So I guess as long as it takes to make me look more natural," Nicole answered as she rolled her eyes.

"You really do have beautiful skin," the salesgirl commented as she cradled Nicole's face between her hands and turned it from side to side. "Tight little pores and as smooth as a newborn's behind."

"Our mother," Nicole announced, "was from Charleston." As if women from South Carolina had the corner on good skin. The young salesgirl nodded politely as she applied a layer of gloss to Nicole's mouth.

"I really don't care for this apricot gloss," Nicole said as she grabbed a tissue to wipe her lips. "How about some dark red like this one."

"I think the apricot would be more pleasing with your coloring," Daisy said smoothly as she took the red lipstick from Nicole.

"It reminds me of a bridesmaid dress," Nicole sulked. "A horrible 70's bridesmaid dress. I don't want orange lips. My mouth looks like a big orange saucer."

"Nicole," Jessie said patiently. "You need to be nice and let this young lady do her job. She is a professional, after all."

"But . . ." Nicole tried to protest.

"No buts" Jessie cut her off. "I stood in that dressing room and was measured by Grandma Moses and tried on every freakish bra you pulled off the rack. Hell, I even tried on a leopard print water bra. Now you are going to sit here and let this very nice woman show you how to apply makeup so you don't look like the side show at the circus."

Stunned by Jessie's outburst, Nicole leaned back in the chair and never said a word as Daisy applied the apricot lip gloss for the third time. She never said a word when the bronze eye shadow was applied and never said a word when Daisy rang up her new cosmetics for $600. The girls left the store and headed to the car.

"I think we need to get some lunch," Jessie said.

"I think we need to get some martinis," Nicole answered.

"Let's go to that cute little bistro down on the beach. I heard they have a great lunch menu," Jessie answered.

"I hope they have a dark corner we can sit in so no one can see my orange saucer lips," Nicole pouted as she put on her sunglasses.

"I think your lips look fine," Jessie tried to assure her.

"Fine if you're doing an orange popsicle commercial," Nicole answered.

"I don't know why this bothers you so much," Jessie said.

"I think your makeup looks great. Mom would have loved it."

"Yeah, I'm sure she would have," Nicole answered. "This is the same mother that dressed me up in an orange pleated skirt with black and white saddle shoes for my first day of school."

"Maybe that's why you don't like orange," Jessie laughed.

"Very funny. Do you remember what you wore the first day of school?" Nicole asked.

"It wasn't important," Jessie answered.

"It was a purple and green plaid dress with little purple flowers on the collar," Nicole said. "You were so cute."

"How can you remember something so insignificant?" Jessie asked.

"I have photos," Nicole whispered as she leaned toward Jessie.

"Oh my God" Jessie said horrified. "She took pictures?"

"You know how mom was. Documented every little outfit we wore so she could have a good laugh at our expense. And even from her grave she has provided herself with a sideshow. I bet she is the most popular person up in heaven keeping everybody laughing at our expense," Nicole laughed.

"And I bet she is mighty proud of my new boobs," Jessie said as she pushed her chest out, "and your new orange lips."

It took Nicole a few weeks to get the hang of her new grooming procedure every morning, but Jessie fell right into enjoying her newfound boobs. She wore tank tops every chance she got. Nicole found it quite entertaining to watch the men gawking at her sister everywhere they went, and it was even more amusing to watch Jessie pretend she didn't notice.

One Saturday morning Nicole arrived at the breakfast table in an exceptionally foul mood.

"What's the matter with you?" Jessie asked.

"I'm sick of this game mother is making us play," Nicole huffed. "Making us do all of these silly things every month. What's the point of it?"

Jessie raised her eyebrows but said nothing, waiting for one of Nicole's rants to begin. Oh God, Jessie thought, I am so not in the mood for this.

"I mean honestly," Nicole snapped a slice of bread in the toaster "she's had us doing charity work, looking for our inner goddess while we're attempting a belly dance, and doing a makeover, among other things. Really," her voice rose "what is the point of it all?"

Again, Jessie said nothing as she sipped her coffee.

"Well?" Nicole demanded. "Don't you have anything to say?"

Jessie took a deep breath and looked pointedly at her sister. "What do you want me to say, Nicole? That there is no point to it? That mother simply wanted us to jump through these hoops for the hell of it?"

Nicole stared at her sister, fuming as she pulled the crispy bread from the toaster. "In your infinite wisdom and pragmatic view of the world, I want you to explain to me why we have to do all of these things."

"Because," Jessie said "it is what mother told us to do. And if you can't see the purpose of each and every letter she has left for us, then you are even more pathetic than she realized."

"Pathetic?" Nicole shouted. "You think I'm pathetic? In six months she has had us do the most ridiculous things and I've done every damn thing she's asked us to do." Tears welled up in her eyes as she continued. "Are you telling me that you understand why she's making us do all of this?"

"Yes" Jessie's voice was tight. "I do understand. I get it."

"Well" Nicole hissed "why don't you just explain it to your pathetic sister?"

Jessie stood then, and walked to face her sister as she spoke. "She wants us to know each other and love each other, Nicole. And if you can't get even that much out of the past six months, then I don't know what to tell you." Jessie and Nicole stared at each other then Jessie turned and walked out the door.

After an hour, Nicole came out to the porch and sat quietly next to her sister. "I'm sorry," she said. "I guess I'm just having a hard time with this. Some days more than others."

Jessie nodded as she continued to watch the ocean, but stayed silent.

"I miss London, I miss my friends...hell, I miss my life, Jess."

They sat silently for a few moments, and then Jessie turned to Nicole. "Do you really regret having to be here?"

Nicole shook her head. "Of course not. But I do miss what my life was like before all of this."

"Me, too," Jessie said. "But we've gone through six months now, and we've had some really good times, haven't we?"

"We have," Nicole agreed, then added "but my inner goddess isn't getting much practice."

"I heard Jake's friend Matt is coming up from Florida in a

few weeks" Jessie said. "I think when you meet Matt your inner goddess will be right back on track."

Nicole looked inquisitively at her sister. "Who is Matt?"

"Oh don't worry, Nicole" Jessie smiled. "I'll give you plenty of time to do your hair and make-up before he arrives."

"You'd better," Nicole said with a twinkle in her eye, "because my inner goddess is dying to come out and play. And by the way" she added "have you heard from Jake lately?"

Jessie shifted in her chair. "Sure, of course. I hear from him a lot."

"Look" Nicole started "I know you think that getting involved with him would be a bad idea, but I see how the two of you look at each other. I see the way he looks at you when you're working at the ranch. That man is head-over-heels in love with you and he's not going to wait forever."

"But what if it doesn't work out?" Jessie said.

"And what if it does?" Nicole countered. "What if you two are meant to be together and you pass it up because you're afraid of failure with him? C'mon, Jess...do you stay in the house on a cloudy day because you're afraid of getting wet?"

Jessie rolled her eyes. "It's a little more complicated than that."

"No" Nicole sat up. "It's not. You're making it complicated."

Jessie bit her lip as she listened to her sister. "I am crazy about him," she confessed.

Nicole shook her head. "Finally, you admit it. So why don't you let him know?"

"I think he knows."

"So let him know that you know and that you're ready to do something about it." Jessie glanced toward Nicole but didn't answer.

"Okay" Nicole threw her hands in the air. "You leave me no choice."

Jessie eyed her sister. "What are you talking about?"

Nicole picked up the phone. "I'll have to call Jake myself and tell him you just might be ready to take the next step."

"Oh stop your dramatics" Jessie said as she snatched the phone. "I'll talk to him next time I see him."

"Well don't wait too long" Nicole harped. "That man has already waited long enough."

They watched the sun rise higher in the sky. Talking came so easily now the girls could barely recall their awkwardness of just a few months ago.

"So tell me," Jessie said, "are you grateful for anything we've done over the past few months?"

Nicole glanced at her sister, then walked toward the railing to peer at the water. "Of course," she said. "I'm grateful for a lot of things. Mostly," she turned her back to the water and looked at Jessie, "getting to know you better. I thought because of the ranch that you'd become someone different, but you're not. You're still my little sister...still Jessie."

Jessie nodded and smiled. "I guess I thought the same about you. That you'd changed into a person I wouldn't like."

"But you do like me?"

Jessie laughed. "Of course I like you. I'd forgotten how much fun you could be. Besides," she said, "would I take belly dancing lessons with someone I don't even like?"

"Know what else I'm grateful for?" Nicole asked. "I'm grateful that you didn't see the little accident Higgins had on the living room rug. But, I might note, I'd be really grateful to see a few more men on this island."

Jessie raised her eyebrows "Why, Nicole," she smiled "I

thought you didn't particularly care about meeting anyone."

"Well, you did mention someone named Matt."

"And?"

"And it just got me thinking that I haven't been out on a date since I came to this godforsaken island." Jessie took the opportunity to tease her sister. "Well, I could call Jake for you. I'm sure he'd be more than happy to come and service you."

Nicole sipped her coffee. "I'm sure he would much rather service you. Besides" she looked squarely at Jessie "I want to hear more about this Matt person."

"Oh, I've only met him once. Can't tell you much about him, but he seemed nice enough."

"Hmmm," Nicole squinted and studied her sister "why do I get the feeling you're not telling me everything."

Jessie stood to walk toward the kitchen. "Maybe," she said, "I'd rather let you find out about him on your own."

Sunday morning had Gus and Higgins in a barking frenzy. Jessie walked to the window and saw Mr. Justice coming up the walk.

"Good morning," she said as she opened the door. "What brings you all the way out to Pawley's Island, Mr. Justice?"

"Please," he said as he stopped to catch his breath "call me Sonny."

"Okay, Sonny," she held the door open and ordered the dogs the sit. "Please come in and have a cup of coffee."

"Delighted to," he smiled as he entered the kitchen. "A cup of coffee sounds like just what I need." As Jessie poured the coffee, the attorney looked around the kitchen.

"My goodness," he smiled, "this place hasn't changed much since your sweet grandmother lived here."

"No," Jessie placed the coffee in front of him. "Nicole and I talked about doing some decorating, but honestly," she smiled, "it would be so hard to get rid of any of Grandmother's things. There are so many memories and wonderful feelings attached to just about everything in this house."

"But new curtains wouldn't hurt," Nicole said as she came down the stairs. "Good morning, Sonny," she smiled. "What brings you to Pawley's Island? You wouldn't be checking up on us, would you?" she smiled.

Sonny let out a hearty laugh. "No, I don't think either of you need a babysitter. I had some business with Willie Jones and just thought I'd make sure you girls are getting along on the Island."

"Well, as a matter of fact," Nicole said as she poured herself a cup of coffee, "Willie came by just the other day to bring us some shrimp and grits."

"He's a fine old gentleman," Sonny offered. "Been living on this island his entire life. And," he continued, "he's quite a character."

Jessie smiled. "He keeps the local flavor alive, that's for sure."

"Sonny," Nicole offered sweetly, "Could we offer you some breakfast?"

The lawyer raised his eyebrows. "Well, I think that would be mighty kind of you."

Jessie understood the look that Nicole flashed her. It was one thing to be polite, but Jessie knew that Nicole had no idea how to cook an entire breakfast for a guest. Unless, of course, a bowl of cold cereal was the only thing expected.

"Nicole" Jessie smiled "it's my turn to do breakfast. Why don't you and Sonny sit on the porch while I whip something up."

Alone in the kitchen, Jessie quickly cut up some fresh

strawberries and made a batch of pancakes. She placed the dishes, utensils, and napkins on a tray and called to Nicole.

"Thank you" Nicole whispered as she picked up the tray. "I never thought Sonny would say yes, but look at him," she peeked over her shoulder. "It doesn't look like he's said no to many meals." Jessie followed her sister to the balcony and placed the tray of pancakes, strawberries, and syrup down as Nicole set the table.

"Well" Sonny sounded surprised "I guess you ladies have been busy learning your way around the kitchen."

"I must admit," Jessie sat down and offered Sonny the plate of pancakes, "some of mom's letters have caught us off guard."

"Oh?" Sonny wasn't shy scooping the strawberries onto a healthy plate of pancakes. "I knew about the letters, but I never knew what your sweet mother had written. And," he put his hand up, "I surely don't mean for you to discuss them with me."

Nicole's eyes narrowed. "Well, she left us certain...challenges that we should try to meet."

"Did she?" Sonny commented absently as he focused on the plate of food before him. "Jessica, these are the most delightful plate of flapjacks I have had in quite some time."

"Thank you," she said as she glanced at her sister. "So you never knew what mom wrote in these letters?"

"No," Sonny smiled. "She didn't share the details with me." He paused and set his fork down. "Your mother did tell me that she felt she had never been strict enough and that she had let the family money have too much influence over both of you."

Neither Nicole nor Jessie believed him for a minute. If Sonny Justice didn't know what was in the letters, what was he doing here all the way from Charleston? Surely he could find breakfast in one of the city's restaurants. No, they both thought, Jethro A. "Sonny" Justice had 8 million reasons to check on them and neither Jessie nor Nicole doubted it for a second.

"Now your mother was a darling woman, but like I've said before, she had a bit of a devilish streak in her." He quickly raised his hand, "Please don't misunderstand me," he said. "I'm not saying Sara was mean, but she could certainly test a person's armor."

Nicole and Jessie exchanged a knowing glance. "I'll bet she could" Jessie smiled. "She's certainly been testing ours."

"Really" Sonny said as he sipped his coffee. "I trust things haven't been too difficult for either of you."

"Oh, if slumming in a thrift store with homeless people is your idea of fun," Nicole ignored Jessie's glare, "then no, it hasn't been difficult. On the other hand," she continued, "we have gotten to visit mother's sister a few times, and that has been a treat. She's quite senile, you know."

"Nicole!" Jessie barked. "Gert is not senile."

"She has bowling balls planted in her garden" Nicole stated.

"She's colorful, not senile" Jessie insisted.

"What of these letters? Have you opened all of them?" Sonny asked.

"No," Nicole said. "We open one every time we're in the mood for a little torture."

Jessie glared at her sister. "It hasn't been so bad." She turned to the bulky attorney as he wiped his chin. "Mother has taught us some valuable lessons from her letters."

"Would you like to share some of your new-found knowledge?" he urged.

"Well," Jessie started "in the big picture, I think mother has shown us a new appreciation for the wonderful life we've been given."

"How so?" Sonny asked, genuinely interested. "Could I bother you for another cup of this delicious coffee?" Sonny held his cup toward Nicole.

Nicole spoke as she filled the cup with fresh coffee. "Since Jessie and I took mother's advice on physical fitness, we walk the beach at least once or twice a week, don't we, Jess."

Her sister nodded and picked up the summary of lessons for the attorney. "When we worked at the thrift store, we were amazed that some of these people have so little yet they are such proud people. It's like" Jessie searched for the words "like they have such an appreciation for what they have. There's no self-entitlement there," she paused. "The people with the least in their lives seem to be the most humble."

Sonny raised his eyebrows and nodded appreciatively at their words. "When we visited Gert," Nicole continued, "we had that horrible hurricane. We were very lucky that we were spared the worst of it, but Jessie and I realized how few relatives we have."

Jessie nodded and continued. "We've spoken to Gert several times over the past few months, and I'm sure we'll visit her again and again now."

"I'm very pleased to hear that. And I'm certain," he patted Jessie's hand, "that your mother would be very pleased with the appreciation you young ladies have come upon."

They closed the door after Sonny left and looked at each

other. "Doesn't know what's in those letters, my ass," Nicole said flatly. "He's about as dumb as a fox."

"No wonder mother picked him as a lawyer," Jessie added. "He could probably charm the skin off a snake."

"Well," Nicole said lightly "at least he knows that we're not complete condescending bitches with no appreciation for the other half."

"No," Jessie offered her sister a half smile. "Not completely."

"We've been raised with privilege," Nicole sniffed. "Of course we have more breeding than some people."

"Yes we do," Jessie sighed at her sister's attitude, "but it doesn't make us better people just because we've been blessed with money."

"Of course we're not better people," Nicole countered. "Just better looking people."

"Speaking of better looking," Jessie countered, "we have an appointment at the spa tomorrow morning. Would you like to go down to the beach this afternoon?"

Nicole's face lit up and she headed for the stairs. "I can be ready to go in fifteen minutes."

As they lay on the beach, Jessie thought they would probably be opening another letter that evening, and mentioned it to Nicole.

"Well when we do, we'll be drinking a martini made out of the best vodka, wearing a wonderful new outfit, and looking tanned and fabulous."

"Yes" Jessie laughed. "With all of that, I can face anything mother throws our way."

Little did they suspect as they settled on the deck later that evening what was in store for them as they began to read the letter.

My Darlings,

I've never given a moment to concern myself over your independence. I know each of you is strong-willed and determined to live life on your own terms.

On the one hand, being independent in a gifted life has blessed you with certain privileges not afforded the majority of people in this world. You have never had to struggle for even basic things as some have had to struggle for their very existence.

On the other hand, those very blessings have diminished your need for self-sufficiency. Sometimes a bit of a struggle builds character. I have often wondered how you girls would do without all of the trimmings your family's wealth has afforded you.

Perhaps a few days in the wilderness would give you an appreciation for some of the things you take for granted. Things like a roof over your heads, electricity, hot running water, and a fine meal.

I'm confident you will come to understand the true meaning of self-sufficiency by taking a little camping trip together.

And no, Nicole, I have not lost my mind.

Your loving Mother

CHAPTER 11
DOES PORCSHE MAKE A CANOE?

Jessie and Nicole sat perfectly still, stunned at this new request their mom had made.

"This one must be a joke," Jessie stated with a hint of a smile.

"Joke or no joke, I am not spending one minute in the wilderness," Nicole said indignantly, then turned seriously to her sister.

"Did mom have dementia?" she asked.

Jessie laughed at her sister's exasperated search for a way out. "I already told you mom wasn't senile."

"But she must have been," Nicole pleaded. "She could not have raised us the way she did and then throw us into the woods to fend for ourselves."

"I think I understand her," Jessie said.

"Well please explain it to me," Nicole demanded, "because the only thing I understand is that mom wants us to go into the woods, get eaten by a mountain lion, and join her in the afterlife."

"Really," Jessie said, "I think you're being a bit sensational. It doesn't sound that bad."

Nicole turned to her sister with a horrified look. "Are you serious? Are you actually considering doing this thing? Going out to live in the woods?"

Jessie propped her feet up on the railing and pulled her visor down. "Oh, c'mon, Nicole. It would be so much fun – building a campfire, roasting marshmallows. We could even tell a ghost story or two."

Nicole stomped across the deck and stood directly in front of her sister. "Let me tell you this one time. I am not – I repeat NOT – going to spend one second in the woods. Mankind spent thousands of years learning to stand on two feet so he could walk out of the woods and I am not going to walk back into them."

The squabble continued on and off over the next week. Jessie was trying to drop gentle hints about a camping trip and with each mention Nicole seemed more adamant about not going anywhere near the woods.

One evening, after an especially successful belly dancing class, Nicole was pouring Jessie and herself a fresh martini and she suddenly relented.

"Jessie," she started cautiously, "do you honestly think mom intended for us to spend any substantial amount of time in the woods? I mean," she continued, "perhaps she just wants us to go for a walk down a lovely tree lined trail."

Jessie looked at Nicole as she spoke. "Nicole, I don't think that's what mom had in mind."

Nicole moved her deck chair closer to the rail and peered out at the sea for a moment. When she spoke, her voice was low and compliant. "Okay, I'll do it."

Jessie turned to her sister, surprised at the turn of events. "What changed your mind?"

"I don't know. Maybe just thinking about mom and what it is she's trying to teach us. Maybe it's the money...I don't know. I just..." she hesitated, "I just feel like if this is what mom needed to tell us, she must have had a good reason."

"Beyond the fact that she's somewhere watching us and having a great laugh at our expense?" Jessie asked.

"Will we have to kill anything to eat?" Nicole's sincerity was more than Jessie could handle.

"Is that what you're afraid of?" she laughed.

"Well, I've never killed anything. Not even a spider. If we don't kill something, what will we eat?" Nicole paused. "Besides, I don't know if I could kill something and then eat it."

Jessie howled at the mental picture of her sister skulking around the woods in her designer clothes, gun in hand, trying to shoot a wild turkey. "It will be nothing like that, I promise you. We'll bring our own food to cook and eat."

"What about bathing?" Nicole seemed on the verge of tears and Jessie felt a stab of guilt at the enjoyment she was taking at her sister's expense.

"We'll bathe in the river – with soap and shampoo and everything" Jessie assured her.

"Will the water be deep?" Nicole asked.

Jessie suddenly recalled their early childhood years, with Nicole sitting on the side of the lake watching while Jessie splashed and played for hours, all the while pleading with her sister to join the fun. But Nicole never would. Jessie turned to her sister and studied her intently. "You can't swim, can you, Nicole?"

She sniffed, trying to muster some dignity. "London isn't like America. There aren't pools in every back yard. Hell," she snorted, "most people don't even have back yards," she paused. "And the weather isn't lovely like it is here."

"Well when we go into the river to clean up," Jessie promised, "I'll make sure it isn't very deep."

Jessie and Nicole planned their trip for the 15th of the month. Nicole insisted on a weekend outing so there would be more people around in case they got in trouble. Jessie planned their camping gear needs, their food supply and their timing. Nicole planned her wardrobe.

A few days before their trip, sitting in their favorite spot on the porch, Jessie dropped the bomb on Nicole.

"I've invited a couple of friends to join us," she announced nonchalantly.

Nicole glanced at her sister. "Friends? I didn't know we had any friends here close enough to take on a field trip."

"Well, you know Jake well enough."

Nicole began to feel a strange sensation building in the pit of her stomach as Jessie continued. "I told you about Jake's friend Matt. He's up from Florida, and he called about getting together with us," Jessie continued with false confidence. "I told him about the camping trip and he thought that sounded like great fun."

Nicole's stomach was now in a tight knot and she pulled herself up to her full height. "Jessie," she tried to sound patient, "are you telling me that you have now invited an audience?"

Jessie sunk deeper into her chair. "They'll be a big help to us, don't you think?"

Nicole pondered this for only a second. "No," she said emphatically, "I don't see them as a big help to us." She lowered her sunglasses and glared at Jessie. "I see them as a couple of chaps who will have the time of their life laughing at a pair of sisters making complete fools of themselves." Nicole continued to gain steam with her tirade. "I see them enjoying a good peek at us as we try to bathe in a fish filled river, eating all of our food, having a good laugh during the day, and trying to crawl into our tent in the evening for a quick feel."

"Nicole" Jessie started but her sister was in high gear now.

"And I see you and I paddling down the river, hair wrapped in a kerchief, and filthy with sweat from fighting with the canoe paddles. I cannot believe," Nicole declared defiantly, "that you have actually arranged a blind date for me on what will likely be the most wretched weekend of my entire life."

Jessie let her sister rant on for several more minutes, until she finally seemed to be losing her fury. "First of all, this isn't a blind date. It's just a couple of friends."

"Friends? You don't even know this other guy." Nicole protested. "What if he turns out to be a psychopath? We'll have nowhere to ditch him. We'll be stuck in the woods with a psychotic killer."

"Oh, don't be ridiculous. I've know Jake for years and he's not the type of man whose best friend is a psycho."

Nicole pouted silently, still glaring at Jessie as she continued.

"His name is Matt – does that sound like a psychopath name?"

"Neither did Ted or Jeffrey, but look at what those guys did. Hey," she sat upright, "didn't Ted Bundy like to go camping?"

Jessie rolled her eyes, determined to get her sister to see the up side to this news, but before she could say anything, Nicole started again.

"What is this guy....Mike or Matt or whatever his name is? I'll bet he's some kind of lumberjack type – or some mountain climbing, outdoorsy freak."

"Actually," Jessie said, "Matt owns a couple of Porsche dealerships in South Florida."

"Good," Nicole pouted, "ask him if Porsche makes a canoe that we can drive down the river."

"So it's okay?" Jessie offered.

"Of course it's not okay," she fussed, "but since you've already invited them, it seems I don't have a choice. Oh," she feigned, "I will be so happy when this entire ordeal is over and I can return to a normal life in London."

The morning of the overnight canoe trip started poorly. The girls woke at 6:00 AM to a light drizzle and even though the weather forecast called for clearing sunny skies, Nicole came downstairs looking as foul as the weather.

"I've decided to stay home," she announced.

Jessie had been expecting this and was well prepared. "Okay," she agreed, "I'll stay home, too. We can scour the want ads together to find jobs."

"Oh, piss off," Nicole said. "You know I have to go."

"Well then what are you whining about?" Jessie asked.

"It's raining – you know how my hair frizzes in the rain."

"Stop going on about your hair and help me pack this cooler."

Nicole pouted but went about packing for the trip as though she'd been doing this all of her life. Jessie was amazed at how she packed the less needed items first and those they would need quickly on the top. Of course, what Nicole considered "necessary" was a first-rate bottle of champagne.

Jake and Matt arrived at 7:30, and Nicole was immediately taken by Matt's self-confident but low-key demeanor. His deep, raspy voice and husky good looks didn't hurt either, she noted. Introductions were made all around, the car was packed, and the ride to the outpost was lively and easy.

Jessie's skills at canoeing were limited, but compared to Nicole she was a pro. Nicole's first challenge came with stepping into the canoe. Matt gently guided her, one foot at a time, and she found herself seated inside the boat, oblivious to the fact that her movements resembled an alpaca trying to maneuver through a minefield.

"I've never been in a canoe," she said, stating the obvious.

"Really?" Matt smiled. "I wouldn't have guessed."

"Thank you," she said demurely, and smoothed her humidity soaked hair.

"So," Matt said as he handed her a paddle, "do you know what to do?"

Nicole took the paddle, looking confused and taken back that she was expected to 'do' anything. "Not really," she said.

Matt laughed and reached for the paddle from Nicole's hand. "Just kidding," he said, and with one swift movement they were away from the bank and on their way. Nicole was silent for the first few moments, awed by the quiet morning mist that still surrounded them. She took in the beauty of the lush green hillside and closed her eyes to soak in the solitude of the morning.

"So you live in London?" Matt's deep voice brought her back.

"Yes, I have since I was a teenager."

"How do you like the states?" he asked.

Nicole hesitated and thought about it for a moment. "I'm not really sure yet," she said. "The past few months haven't really been what I would call typical."

Suddenly, Nicole's eyes caught the eruption of water ahead of them. "OH MY LORD!" she shouted. "It's a waterfall. We're going to drown! Jessie," she yelled across to her sister, "you said there wouldn't be anything like this."

Whether Matt was alarmed or amused by Nicole's sudden panic, she didn't know – and honestly didn't care. She was consumed by the vision of being yanked out of the little wooden boat, plummeting down the falls, and being pulled underwater as the air was being sucked out of her lungs.

"Please go a different way," she said, panic filling her voice. Matt easily maneuvered the canoe to the left, toward an alcove of trees. Jessie and Jake took his lead and were soon alongside them in knee-deep water. Matt lassoed a rock to secure the canoe and used a bungee to tether Jake's boat to theirs.

Nicole was so shaken she began to cry. "Mom wants us to die, I'm sure of it now, Jessie. She wants us to join her in the afterlife so she won't be so lonely."

The other three glanced at each other, trying to hide their amusement. Matt took Nicole's hand and looked into her eyes as though she were the only person on earth that mattered to him. "Nicole," he started, "that's not a waterfall. It's called a rapids. It's just shallow water moving over rocks. We'll go around it and we'll be fine."

Nicole suddenly had total faith in Matt. She knew her life was in his hands now and for some reason she trusted that he would let no harm come to her. "Okay?" he asked.

"Just give me a minute?" she asked, suddenly embarrassed by her alarming outburst.

"Take as long as you need," he said soothingly. Jessie handed Nicole a bottle of juice and she sipped it. "What is this?" she asked.

"A mimosa," Jessie smiled. "I thought you'd be needing it to calm your nerves."

"It's lovely...thank you." She took another sip from the bottle and looked around at her companions. "I'm so sorry," she said.

"Hey," Jake offered, "didn't your sister tell you about her first time out?"

Nicole eyed Jessie. "No," she said, "as a matter of fact she didn't. But I'm sure it's a delightful tale that we'd all love to hear."

Jessie eyed Jake with good humor. "Oh, go ahead," she laughed. "Tell them if you must."

"Well," Jake started, "let me put it this way. At least you made it into the canoe."

Nicole howled with laughter. "You fell in? You didn't even make it into the boat?"

"Jake wasn't as chivalrous as Matt," Jessie good-naturedly tried to defend herself. "He didn't help me into the canoe. He just jumped in and picked up the oars."

With the ice broken, Nicole said she was okay to continue, but as they neared the churning water, she grew quiet. Matt tried to soothe her nerves but she heard nothing except the voice inside her own head screaming at her to jump now and hope for the best. As the canoe wobbled and jerked across the rapids, Nicole's eyes grew wide, but before she could react, they were once again sliding smoothly across the calm water.

They stopped for a lunch of salad and sandwiches at a beautiful landing area. The trees formed a canopy that shaded them from the sun that had now risen overhead, and the velvety grass cushioned them where they'd spread a blanket. Nicole had relaxed considerably and was now animated and entertaining. Jessie hadn't seen her sister this happy since their childhood. Thank God for the mimosas, Jessie thought.

"What time do we need to finish for the day?" she asked. Matt was obviously impressed by Nicole's determination to finish the trip, even though he was certain she was terrified by the entire ordeal.

"Well," he started, looking at Jake for confirmation; "I'd think another couple of hours should do it for today. We don't want to wait too long to start camp."

Jake chimed in teasingly, "We have to be zipped in our tents before the bears come out."

Jessie laughed but Nicole only smiled, looking to Matt for comfort." No bears," he assured her. And as he turned to open the cooler, he said under his breath "None that I've ever seen, anyway."

As he looked at Nicole he laughed at her uneasiness. "Kidding again" he assured her.

The afternoon started easily enough, and Nicole even offered to take one of the oars if Matt would show her what to do. A quick lesson and Nicole was paddling her side of the canoe with relative ease.

For about 5 minutes.

"What's that?" she asked.

"More rapids," he answered easily. "Think you can handle it?"

"Do you?" Nicole countered, her voice sounding more confident than her mind was telling her to be.

"Just follow my instruction. You'll need to move the paddle from one side to the other to keep us straight," he instructed. "When I say 'left', you paddle that side, when I say 'right', paddle on the other side. Got it?"

Nicole nodded enthusiastically, anxious to show that she was facing one of her great fears. As the canoe began to wobble, Matt called "Left" and she followed his coaching. He suddenly shouted "Right" and Nicole dropped her paddle into the water, leaned over to quickly retrieve it, and the canoe promptly tipped to the left and went over. Nicole screamed for her life, arms flailing, legs thrashing, her head bobbing like a buoy in a hurricane. Matt scooped her up by the arms, and pushed her toward a rock that was just inches away. She clung to the rock as

Matt went to recover the canoe, and she noticed the water was only up to his waist.

Embarrassed by her reaction to being dumped in shallow water as though she'd been thrown into the ocean, Nicole climbed onto the rock and watched as Matt recovered their gear. Jessie and Jake had maneuvered their canoe through the rapids and were paddling toward the debris floating downstream. They quickly recovered a cooler and a tent and then guided their vessel toward the bank to wait for Nicole and Matt.

"Nicole," she heard Jessie shouting, "Are you hurt?"

Nicole waved at her sister to indicate she was fine. Matt pushed the canoe to Jessie and Jake, then went to retrieve Nicole, who sat huddled on the rock like a forsaken mermaid.

"Matt," she said tearfully, "I am so sorry. I just…"

"Hey," he said with heart wrenching sincerity, "I didn't want to sleep in a dry tent tonight."

"Oh no," Nicole said as she closed her eyes, "the tent got soaked."

"As did our sleeping bags, our food, and," he studied her with a devious grin, "that life jacket you're wearing definitely got a soaking."

Nicole glanced down at the orange vest and the vision of herself flailing about popped into her head. "Oh" was all she could muster.

With all of their gear stowed back into the canoe, the group set off again and the rest of the afternoon went seamlessly.

And then it was time to set up camp.

The campground was arranged with several sections of flat, grassy areas separated by clumps of trees. Each camping area had a fire pit, a picnic table, and a large drum for trash. Away from the main area - much to Nicole's horror - were portable toilets. Not wanting to make a fool of herself again, Nicole kept silent but realized using a toilet in the woods was something she had not thought about.

"Nicole," Matt called to her "can you help me spread out the tent and the sleeping bags to dry them?"

"Since I'm the reason they're wet, I guess that's the least I could do."

Jessie went about her task as though she'd been raised in a campground, knowing exactly what to do and how to do it. Nicole felt a bit helpless and was pleased that Matt, who was growing more admirable by the hour, kept her busy with chores and assignments.

With the tents set up, Jessie turned to Nicole "Do you want to grab a bath before it gets too late?"

"In the river?" Nicole questioned with a bit of desperation in her voice.

"Yes, in the river," Jessie answered patiently. "We talked about this, remember?"

"I saw fish in there," Nicole protested half-heartedly. Nicole glanced at Jake and Matt, who were pretending not to listen to the exchange. Jessie's patience was wearing a bit thin after the rigors of a day in the canoe. "Of course there are fish in there...it's a RIVER."

Nicole pouted for a flash, then whispered to her sister. "Do we have to be naked?"

Jessie rolled her eyes. "Only if you want to be. I'm going to change into my swimsuit." Jessie took her small pack and ducked into the tent with Nicole following like a child imitating her parent's lead.

Zipped protectively in the tent, the girls began to get ready. Nicole turned her back to her sister, and Jessie began to understand her sister's typical British modesty. Jessie finished and turned to find Nicole still fully clothed.

"What are you waiting for?"

"I don't get naked in front of other women," she stated. "It's not natural."

Jessie stared at her sister. "Unbelievable" she said, and left the tent.

Nicole zipped the closure and laid out her swimsuit, then began to undress. As she pulled off her shorts, her foot snagged the edge of the tent and she tumbled awkwardly into the side of the canvas. She righted herself and kicked at her foot until it freed itself from the seam of the tent. From outside of the tent Jessie, Matt and Jake were watching Nicole's rigorous struggle. To the three of them, she looked like a rabbit trying to beat its way out of a canvas sack and the sight was more than they could stand.

"What are you doing in there?" Jessie called.

Collecting herself as she wiggled unceremoniously into her swimsuit, Nicole answered breathlessly, "Be right there."

Jake reached over and patted Matt on his shoulder. "You're a good sport, buddy," he said as he shook his head. "I don't know if I could have as much patience."

Just then Nicole unzipped the tent and stepped out wearing a short silk robe over her swimsuit. Jessie stared in amazement. "We're not going to a spa, honey, we're bathing in a river. What's with the silk wrap?"

"Oh," Nicole smiled, "It might be chilly when we get out of the water."

Jessie rolled her eyes and gave Matt a sympathetic glance. "Well" she stood up "let's get going."

The four of them walked the short distance to the edge of the river. Jake and Matt stepped into the water and came up with a shiver.

"Pretty chilly," Jake yelled to the girls on the shore. "I think you'll need more than that little jacket when we're done."

Matt extended his hand to Nicole as she stepped into the cool water. "Can we bathe quickly?" Nicole asked, "This isn't exactly how I'm used to freshening up."

After a quick dip the foursome walked back to the camp. Nicole tucked her overnight bag under her arm and headed for the bathrooms. "Be back in a jiff," she called over her shoulder as she stepped across the field toward the portable commodes.

Matt glanced at Jessie. "Have you prepped her?"

Jessie smiled slyly. "Not exactly."

Jessie looked up just in time to see Nicole running from the port-o-let, arms waving madly and yelling something none of them understood. Matt stood and started toward Nicole. As he reached her, Jessie could see her sister's panicked expression and wondered if a snake or raccoon had found its way into the toilet area and tried to share the space with Nicole.

Jake and Jessie couldn't hear the conversation, so they were left to guess what the trauma was about. They watched as Matt took Nicole by the shoulders. She shook her head and buried it in Matt's shoulder.

"Do you think it was a snake?" Jake asked.

Jessie smiled at him reassuringly. "I've been with Nicole for six months now and I guarantee it was nothing like that."

"Then what do you think the problem is?" Jake asked with quiet concern. "She seems awfully undone just to realize the commode is a hole in the ground that can't be flushed."

Jessie pondered her sister from a distance and watched as Nicole nodded at Matt's obviously reassuring words, then headed back to the bathroom. As Matt approached them, she realized he was laughing.

"Don't tell me," Jessie called to him "she realized there's no electricity."

Matt smiled and nodded. "No place to plug in her hair dryer and some kind of hair straightening device and her hair, it seems, will frizz up like a lion's mane."

Jake and Matt exchanged quick glances, then Jake turned to Jessie. "Are you sure you two are sisters?"

When Nicole returned, hair pulled back in a bulbous ponytail, she politely nodded at Jake and spoke sternly to her sister. "In the tent."

Jessie smiled at Matt and Jake, raised her eyebrows and stood, following Nicole into the tent. Nicole turned abruptly to Jessie.

"Remind me," she said, her voice as tight as a coil, "exactly what having my hair bushed out like a wild animal is teaching me about self-sufficiency." She stopped just as abruptly and Jessie realized the question wasn't rhetorical. Nicole wanted - demanded - an answer.

"I think," Jessie measured her words carefully "that perhaps mom is trying to show us that we can actually survive without the inconsequential things in life."

"Inconsequential?" Nicole repeated. "You think my straightening rod is inconsequential? Look at me!" she said as she pulled at her bulging tail of hair.

"Nicole," Jessie said with sensitive patience "do you honestly believe that out here, on this campground, anyone besides you cares that your hair is frizzy?"

Nicole's bottom lip jutted out and tears welled up and spilled down her cheeks. "What about Matt?" she asked anxiously. "What did he say when he saw me? Did he say I was a horror?"

Not once in the previous months had Jessie seen her sister this downtrodden. Jessie realized her sister had been much more sheltered by their family's affluence and privilege than she herself had been. Jessie had been given the freedom to explore the things that interested her, like her love of animals. She'd had the means to pursue her interests and her mom had been supportive when Jessie laid out her plans to open a service that would cater to sick or retired horses.

Nicole, on the other hand, had been raised to believe that looks and material things were more important than anything. Nicole believed her entire life had to meet with someone's approval. Even her education in fashion had been deemed "acceptable" by their father. Nicole was never encouraged to delve into herself to determine what direction she would like her life to take. If it didn't fit the societal mold, discouragement was the wall Nicole faced.

Now, standing in the fading daylight, hidden by the walls of the tent, Jessie put her hands gently on her sister's shoulders. "Nicole, you are one of the most beautiful and strongest women I have ever met. Whether your hair is frizzy or styled, whether you're in a ballroom or a campground, you're beauty comes from in here," she touched her own chest, "not from clothes or makeup."

Nicole sniffed and swiped at the tears on her face. "Do you think so?"

"Yes," Jessie smiled, "and more importantly, Matt sees that, too."

Nicole smiled appreciatively and nodded, then unexpectedly hugged Jessie. "Okay" she said releasing her sister just as quickly, "I guess we'd better feed the men folk" she laughed.

CHAPTER 12
ROASTED MARSHMALLOWS AND NEW LOVE

They left the tent to find Jake and Matt in the distance, arms loaded with wood, strolling back toward the campsite looking relaxed and animated. Nicole followed Matt's instruction in helping him get the fire lit while Jessie and Jake chatted quietly at the picnic table.

"So," Jessie asked Jake, "what does Matt think about my sister? Drama queen?"

"Not at all," Jake smiled as his fingers brushed a few stray hairs from Jessie's cheek, then continued as if his touch hadn't sent a jolt of electricity through Jessie. "Matt has always been attracted to women who are...." he hesitated, looking for the right word.

"Helpless?" Jessie laughed. "You can go ahead and say it. Nicole is a bit on the needy side."

Jake laughed, conceding the point. "It's the one way we are total opposites."

"Really?" Jessie laughed. "So you like the strong, independent type?"

Jake glanced over toward Nicole and Matt sitting by the fire, laughing and talking and obviously enjoying each other.

"I guess," Jake said haltingly, "I just want a woman who can take care of herself. Someone who wants me in her life, but doesn't necessarily need me in her life." Jake looked at Jessie and said, "Someone like you, Jess."

Taken off guard, Jessie couldn't answer and before she had the chance to collect her thoughts, Matt called over to them. "We're getting a little hungry over here. What about you two?" Jake gave Jessie's hand a quick squeeze and stood up.

"Comin' right up!" he called.

Jessie sat stunned, unable to move. After a moment, Nicole joined her.

"Are you okay, Jessie? You look like you've seen a ghost."

Jessie smiled at her sister and spoke quietly. "Jake just threw me a curveball, I guess."

"What?" Nicole whispered conspiratorially as she sat beside her. "What did he say? Did he propose?"

Jessie laughed at Nicole's usual flair for drama.

"Of course not," she said.

"Well, it wouldn't surprise me if he did. If love had a man's face, it would be Jake."

"What are you talking about?" Jessie frowned at her sister.

"Oh come now," Nicole taunted her. "You can't tell me you are so naïve that you haven't noticed the way he looks at you."

Jessie studied Nicole's face then stood and dismissed her comment with a wave of her hand and walked toward the fire.

"Should be ready in a few minutes," Jake said and patted the spot next to him for Jessie to sit down.

Over dinner, they laughed about the day and told stories about each other's lives. After they'd cleaned up, they decided on what time they would pull out in the morning and said goodnight to all, heading for their tents.

"If something crawls in here during the night," Nicole said as she settled into her sleeping bag, "it had better be Matt."

Jessie laughed quietly. "He's a nice guy."

"Mmmm" was all Jessie could get from her sister before Nicole was sound asleep.

But the peace and quiet of the night did nothing to calm Jessie's mind as she re-lived the past few months with Jake. What could she do? Was she ready to take a chance with Jake? If she couldn't answer that question herself, how could she expect Jake to take the same chance with her. Sleep finally came in the early morning hours and when she heard the men stirring outside the tent, Jessie felt like she had barely gotten any rest.

Jessie stared at Nicole's head, which was now enormous with auburn hair in every direction.

"A bit on the grumpy side this morning?"

"Something was poking me in the ribs all night long." Nicole scuffled with her sleeping bag, reaching underneath and pulling out a pink satin slipper. Jessie snatched it from Nicole and examined the fluffy pom-pom atop it, then looked at the pointed toe.

"Nicole," she started, then thought better. "Never mind, I don't want to know," she said as she tossed the slipper back to Nicole.

The morning went smoothly and by ten o'clock they were back on the river, paddling through smooth water to Nicole's relief. By one o'clock they decided to stop for lunch along the shoreline. As they munched on sandwiches, Matt was telling an animated story about an especially rich, spoiled woman who had recently purchased a top of the line red Porsche for her husband. Once the papers were signed, Matt recognized the name and asked if her husband had just purchased a similar car for their daughter. The look on the woman's face told Matt immediately that they not only didn't have a daughter, but the woman obviously knew nothing about her husband purchasing a Porsche for another woman.

"The deal," Matt said wryly, "went south pretty quickly after that."

Matt gave Nicole a deliberate glance and laughed. "I guess we'll have a few stories to tell about this trip, too."

"Oh go ahead" Nicole blushed. "But remember who you have to share the canoe with for the rest of the day."

Once they were back on land with the car packed, they rode in quiet for a while. Nicole laid her head on Matt's shoulder and dozed. Jessie tried to study Jake's profile as he drove, but he turned and caught her looking at him.

"What?" he asked smiling.

Jessie shook her head. "Nothing," she said defensively.

Jake reached across the seat and took Jessie's hand. "We'll talk another time."

Jessie nodded and wondered what in the world she could possibly say to him. She put her head back and closed her eyes, letting her mind wander. Jessie sighed out loud and felt Jake squeeze her hand again. Nicole lifted her head as the car stopped in the driveway.

"Home, sweet home," Jessie said.

"I hardly think so," Nicole sighed.

When the men had left, Nicole and Jessie settled onto the deck.

"Matt asked if they could come back next weekend," Nicole offered. "I told him that would be nice."

"Hmmm," Jessie said as she sipped her drink, still lost in her thoughts about Jake.

"Do we have to open another one of mother's letters tonight?" Nicole asked, her voice weary and apprehensive.

Jessie glanced at her sister. "A bit anxious for another adventure, aren't you?"

"Well," Nicole said, "we might as well get the torture over with."

The sun was low and the shadows across the deck were long. The sisters sat thoughtfully for a few moments, then Nicole sat upright. "Oh my god!"

"What?" Jessie said looking around.

"What if she has something worse in mind for us? What if" she looked squarely at Jessie, "what if we have to shop at one of those huge warehouse stores for the rest of the year?"

Jessie turned to Nicole and raised her glass in a toast. "Then so be it," she said and downed the rest of her drink as she reached for the envelope.

My darling daughters,

I trust by this time that each of you has gotten to know what unique individuals you have become - something I have always known. I hope that the time you have spent together has provided you with both enjoyment and experiences that you will take with you and treasure for the rest of your lives.

Your Grandmother's house on Pawley's Island has always been a very special place to me. I grew up on this beach, was married on this beach, and died on this beach. So I hope this explains why I wanted you to spend time together at this particular home. I do hope it has become a very special place for both of you as well.

Memories and family are all that's really important in this life. Over the years I know that our family has not always lived under the same roof, or for that matter in the same country.

My darling Nicole, when you went to live with your father in London to attend university, it was the most difficult decision of my life, and many times I had regrets about it. I always knew that it was the right thing to do for you, but my heart never stopped aching. I missed you every day. You have become the smart, vibrant person I knew you would, but even as I write this in my last days on this earth I hope that I made the right choice.

I want you to know how much admiration I have for both of you. I am so proud to have raised such wonderful, generous daughters who were willing to sacrifice a huge part of their personal lives to take care of me when I became sick, and I just want to say THANK YOU – to both of you – for making my life more wonderful than you could ever know.

Jessie, as your mother, I know that you tend to keep your emotions to yourself and this can be an admirable quality. However I wouldn't want you to one day regret any decision that you made when you were just a young girl. The baby that you put up for adoption might one day find her way back into your life, and you need to be able to express your emotions and help her understand why you made the difficult decision that you did. In the end it is your choice whether or not you want to contact her, but if you decide you would like her in your life you can contact Mr. Justice and he will give you more details. Remember that this is your decision and I will always love and respect you.

I am so proud and grateful that I was blessed with two incredibly wonderful daughters. I have loved you both always,

Mother

CHAPTER 13
SECRETS

Nicole reached across the table and squeezed her sister's hand. Jessie sat staring at the waves as they gently washed the sand, gathered up the tiny shells and took them back to sea.

"Jessie," Nicole sat for a moment then spoke to her sister, "I never knew."

Jessie looked thoughtfully at her sister. "No one did. Only mother."

"Do you want to talk about it?"

Jessie nodded, tears welling in her eyes. "I've wanted to talk about it everyday for 21 years. But" a small sob escaped her throat and she struggled to continue. "I couldn't. It was too hard. If I thought about it for too long, it would have consumed me."

Nicole could see her sister's pain but kept silent. Jessie wiped her eyes and continued slowly.

"I was so young - only 16. I didn't even know how to be pregnant, much less how to be a mother." She paused, as though needing her thoughts to catch up with her emotions. "Jeff's parents...that was the father...were horrified. They called me every awful name they could think of. Until" she looked at Nicole "they found out how much money I came from. Then, of course, they wanted a wedding."

"Cows" Nicole commented bitterly.

"But there were too many issues. Jeff was a sweet boy, incredibly good-looking, but we were kids." Jessie looked at Nicole, her eyes begging for understanding from her sister.

Nicole read her sister and complied. "How old was he?"

"Seventeen." Jessie laughed quietly "Could you imagine if I'd gotten married? At sixteen?"

"We're in our thirties and not married, so no" Nicole tried lightly "I can't imagine it at sixteen."

They sat quietly for a few minutes, each in their own thoughts. Nicole finally broke the silence. "And how" Nicole asked in astonishment "did you ever tell mother? Do you remember?"

"I remember everything" Jessie replied "like it was yesterday."

"What did mom say?"

"I had known for about a week. Mom was going to the store and asked me if I needed some 'sanitary pads'. You know mother" Jessie laughed lightly "heaven forbid she should call them Tampax. 'Sanitary pads' or 'female items' - that's all she could bring herself to say."

Nicole smiled and nodded, letting Jessie continue at her own pace. "I guess the look on my face told her. She got this funny expression and said 'Jessica, is there something I need to know'? I started crying in typical teenage fashion and just blurted it out."

"How did she take it?"

Jessie looked at her sister, memories of her mom vivid in her eyes. "She was wonderful, Nicole. She wasn't angry. I'm sure she was terribly disappointed but she never let me see it."

"Sounds like mother" Nicole agreed.

"She sat with me in my bedroom and asked me what I wanted to do. I told her I didn't want a baby but I don't believe in abortion." Jessie suddenly laughed, remembering. "I was so young and foolish; I seriously asked her if she wanted it. That's how naïve I was - I thought I could just give it to her and be done with it!"

Nicole shrugged and took a sip of her martini. "I don't think that's so funny for a sixteen year old back then, given the sheltered life we'd led."

"She asked me about Jeff and I told her about his parents. I never knew what mom did" Jessie glanced at Nicole "but I never heard from Jeff or his parents again."

"Did you love him?" Nicole asked romantically.

Jessie smiled. "I thought I did, but I was sixteen. At 37, I'm still not sure I know what love feels like."

"So how did you decide what to do?" As anxious as she was to hear about this remarkable episode of her sister's life, Nicole waited for Jessie to tell the story on her own terms.

"Again, mom to the rescue. She contacted some people, I went away to school that year in Charlotte, and when it was all over, I signed some papers and came home." She looked at Nicole for her sister's reaction.

"Wow" Nicole said humbly. "And you've never said a word all these years."

Jessie shrugged. "Nicole you had moved to London and I hadn't seen you in over a year. Do you think I'd just call you up one day and say 'Hey, guess what I did on my summer vacation?"

Nicole looked at Jessie and her eyes held a quiet mixture of respect and compassion. "You could have, you know."

The sisters shared a warm look then Nicole poured a fresh batch of martinis and looked toward the beach. "So" she started "are you going to contact Mr. Justice? I knew that chubby little codger had more information than he told us."

Jessie sipped her drink and was quiet for a moment, then shrugged. "I'm not sure. I think that's what mom would have wanted me to do. Otherwise" she looked at Nicole "why would she have brought it up in her letter?"

"Ahhh" Nicole nodded with a smile "even in death, mom reaches out to show us the way in our apparently murky lives."

Jessie and Nicole laughed, then Jessie turned serious again. "Will you stay with me if I go to meet her?"

"Jessie! Of course I will!"

"Is that because you want to be supportive, or because you're dying to see what she looks like?" Jessie asked wryly.

"Well, if I were to be perfectly honest...."

Jessie laughed at her and said "Never mind. I won't force you to confront your honesty. But" she smiled warmly "whatever the reason, thank you."

Jessie stood and started to speak, but as she did, Nicole stood and gave her sister a quick hug. As Nicole went to duck into the house, Jessie tugged on her sister's arm and wrapped her arms warmly around her sister.

When she spoke, her voice cracked with emotion and relief. "If I'd known it was so wonderful to have a sister to live with, I'd have come to London and kidnapped you."

Nicole, accustomed to British formality, was taken off guard but quickly found herself warming to her sister's genuine affection. She hugged Jessie back for a long moment, then stood back and looked her squarely in the eyes.

"What a wonderful idea!"

"To be kidnapped?" Jessie raised her eyebrows.

"To come to London, silly. We'd have a lovely time" Nicole said, her excitement building as she spoke. "When all of these letters from mom are finished, we can tour London with our kinder, gentler personas. We'll even drag our inner goddesses with us. "

Jessie had to laugh at Nicole's enthusiasm. "What about the ranch? I can't expect Jake to continue running it while I'm living it up in London."

"Oh of course. Jake. Let me see..." Nicole feigned thoughtfulness and put her finger to her cheek. "A man that's in love with you, asking him to extend the favor for one more month....hmmm. Yes, yes" she said, "I can see where he wouldn't want you to be happy after all that you've been through."

"Nicole" Jessie smiled softly "can we talk about London another time? I really have more important things on my mind right now."

"I know you do, sweetie, and that's exactly why I'm talking about London."

"To take my mind off of mother's letter? Honestly, Nicole" Jessie said sincerely "that's really sweet but I can't stick my head in the sand any longer."

"What are you going to do?" Jessie looked toward the beach for a moment, then turned back to her sister. "I think I'm going to go upstairs to my room and think about it for a while." She stepped past Nicole and walked slowly up the stairs.

Nicole didn't bring up the subject of her sister having borne a child again that evening, and when the morning light found Jessie already dressed and slicing fruit for her cereal, Nicole knew it had been a sleepless night for her sister.

"I'm going to do it, Nicole" Jessie offered so softly that Nicole wasn't certain at first that she'd heard her.

"Do what?" Nicole asked genuinely.

"See her...meet her. I'm going to call Mr. Justice this morning." Jessie looked hopefully at Nicole, waiting for her reaction. It was surprisingly subdued. Nicole simply raised her eyebrows and slowly nodded her head.

"Aren't you going to say anything?" Jessie asked quickly as she crossed her arms.

"Jess" Nicole sat down with her coffee "do you think you need my approval?"

"Of course not" Jessie answered sharply and turned back to the counter to finish slicing the peaches. For the next few minutes, the only sound was the ticking of their Grandmother's clock and the knife slicing through the peaches.

"Maybe" Jessie finally said in a quiet voice and turned to face her sister. "I know I don't need your approval, Nicole, but it would be nice to know what you think about all of this."

Nicole took a sip from the steaming mug and looked over the rim at her sister. When she took the cup from her lips and placed it on the table, her eyes were locked tenderly with Jessie's.

"What I think" she started softly "is that I'm so sorry I wasn't here for you all those years ago. I'm sorry you had to go through all of that alone, that you had to make that decision alone, and go off to a 'home' by yourself. And I'm sorry you are wondering whether you need my 'approval' to go through another chapter of it, because you surely don't, Jessie."

Nicole stepped forward and took her sister's hand. "You're one of the strongest women I've ever met."

Jessie nodded, barely managing to stay dry-eyed. "Thank you" she said softly. "I'll call Mr. Justice after breakfast."

As the next few days passed, Jessie and Nicole could barely contain themselves. Mr. Justice had arranged for Jessie and Nicole to meet Taylor, Jessie's daughter, in Charleston for lunch, thinking it would be far better to meet in a restaurant where the conversation and busy atmosphere would seem more welcoming than the quiet solitude of their Grandmother's living room.

"What do you think she'll look like?" Nicole asked Jessie as they drove past the beach and onto the highway that led to Charleston. "Was her father a handsome chap?"

"Very" Jessie answered, then smiled "but his father was an awful looking man."

"Really?" Nicole was intrigued by the description. "Awful like mean looking?"

"Awful like road kill" Jessie stated simply.

"Oh God...dreadful." Nicole looked worried. "What if she looks like him?"

"Well" she said lightly "I guess we'll have to give her a

'Nicole Special'. What do you think? A wig? Plastic surgery?"

"Oh Jess!" Nicole laughed at her sister's banter. "Mom told Mr. Justice she was lovely. Does it bother you that mom kept in touch with her all these years and never let you know?"

Jessie pondered the question for a few minutes. "I guess it does in one way. I feel badly" she paused as the traffic slowed to a crawl "that she felt she couldn't share that with me." Jessie glanced at her sister and said "Yet another one of mother's secrets."

They slipped through the traffic in silence for a few minutes, then talked on and off about how the meeting might go. Would it be awkward? Would Taylor decide that she would want Jessie as part of her life? Or worse - that she wouldn't?

The restaurant was half full, and Jessie and Nicole were early. They took a booth against the far wall, wanting a view of the door, but not wanting to be too obvious.

"Nicole" Jessie said suddenly "I'm scared."

"Honey" Nicole patted her sister's hand and giggled nervously "your inner goddess will bring you through this."

"My inner goddess has abandoned me for higher ground" Jessie smiled. "I hope this isn't a mistake."

Without time to answer, Taylor walked through the door and Jessie gasped. "She's here...and she looks like mother."

"Really?" Nicole looked quickly toward the door. "What is she wearing?"

Jessie ignored her sister and stood to greet the young woman that was walking toward them.

"Hi" Jessie said timidly and felt Nicole standing beside her, giving her the moral support she desperately needed.

Taylor stood back for a moment, then reached out to embrace her mother. The relief and emotion flooded over both of them and the tears fell from all eyes.

"Come" Nicole took control "sit and have a drink with us." She paused and said "Are you legal to drink?" she asked as an afterthought.

Taylor laughed lightly "I'm 21. And yes, I would love to have a drink."

The waitress came to the table and they ordered 3 peach martinis. "Grandma drank those" Taylor offered.

"Yes well" Nicole held up her glass "here's to mother...and Grandmother."

Awkwardness had been left at the door, it seemed, as the

women chatted easily through lunch and well into the early afternoon. There were no words like "abandonment" or questions of "why", as Jessie had feared. Taylor had a sweetness about her that was immediately engaging and the ease of the afternoon's meeting had flooded Jessie with relief.

Jessie learned that Taylor had graduated from Clemson this past spring and was taking a year off before graduate school, that she rented a small house in Mount Pleasant, and that she had no current boyfriend.

As they bid goodbye, they confirmed plans for Taylor to come to Pawley's Island the following weekend to stay for a few days.

"Have you ever been to Pawley's?" Nicole asked her as they walked to the car.

"I came to Grandma's funeral." She smiled at the surprise in Jessie's face. "It's how I recognized you when I came in to the restaurant" she offered.

"Well, you'll be coming for a much happier occasion and you'll never want to leave" Nicole said as she waved her hand in the air.

"Grandma loved it, and she was always wanting me to come, but" Taylor sighed heavily "I guess I was always too busy with school and..." she hesitated and looked at Jessie "I guess just busy with my life."

Jessie noted the regret in Taylor's eyes and took her hand. "Don't feel badly, Taylor. Mom loved you, and we have made her very happy today, I'm sure." Jessie smiled and squeezed Taylor's hand. "I can't wait to get to know you."

As they drove back to Pawley's, Nicole chatted happily about how wonderful it was to have a niece, and how much Taylor seemed to be just like Jessie.

"I feel very strange about all of this, Nicole."

She turned to look at Jessie, and Nicole asked what she meant by 'strange'.

"That young woman is my daughter...shouldn't I feel more...." she looked for the words, but Nicole filled in the blanks.

"More motherly?" she asked directly.

"Yes" Jessie fretted and put her palm to her forehead. "Why don't I feel motherly?"

"Give it time, Jessie" Nicole said encouragingly. "You don't know Taylor yet. Besides, it's not exactly a role you've had any practice with."

Jessie began to panic. "What if that never happens? What if I get to know her and don't even like her? How am I supposed to act?"

Nicole took her sister's forearm and squeezed gently. "You're starting to sound like me, Jessie."

Jessie looked at Nicole, eyes filled with panic. "But"

"Jessie" Nicole said firmly "let's talk about something else for a few minutes."

Nicole managed to distract Jessie enough to let the panic attack pass, and soon they were laughing about all of the "lessons" their mom had laid out for them over the past few months.

"I found my inner goddess" Nicole laughed "but I think she drowned on the canoe trip."

"Yeah" Jessie added happily "I think somebody bought mine at the thrift store...but for a bargain price, to be sure."

The following week was filled with plans for Taylor's visit. They'd take her around Pawley's on Saturday and then go to the market and have a quiet dinner at home.

Friday morning Jessie asked Nicole "Do you know how to bake?"

"I'm not even sure what 'baking' is" Nicole quipped. "It has something to do with bread and sweets, doesn't it?"

Jessie rolled her eyes, quite used to her sister's sarcastic wit by now. "Well" Jessie said, "I was thinking of baking an apple pie, what with it being apple season and all."

Nicole eyed her sister suspiciously. "Aren't you taking this motherhood thing a bit too far?"

Jessie laughed, "Oh, I don't know" she said "I could probably find Grandmother's recipe around here."

"Yes" Nicole laughed, "and when you do, be sure to bring it to the local bake shop and ask them if they would be kind enough to whip up a pie using Grandmother's recipe."

Jessie smiled at her sister's taunting. "You don't think I could bake a pie?"

"Oh" Nicole answered, "I know you could bake a pie" she paused "I just don't know if it would resemble anything that ever came out of Grandmother's kitchen."

Jessie pondered this for only a second. "You're right. Let's go to the bakery and see if they have anything good."

Taylor arrived early on Saturday morning amid Nicole's daily beauty treatment. Jessie excused Nicole's appearance and offered to help Taylor carry in her luggage.

"Well" Jessie offered nervously "we've put you in the front bedroom. It has a lovely view of the garden, but if you'd rather"

"Please" Taylor interrupted "wherever you set me up is fine, I'm sure." The women faced each other in the upstairs hallway, a look passed between them that spoke volumes.

"Taylor" Jessie started uncertainly "I think we should go for a walk after you've settled in. I'll show you around the gardens."

As the two walked, Jessie told Taylor about Grandma Mitchell. "She was a very spirited woman," Jessie laughed "a lot like my mother."

"I haven't said this yet" Taylor's voice was soft and sincere "but I'm very happy that you wanted to meet me. I'm certain it can't be easy for you."

Jessie stopped and faced her daughter. "There's so much I want to explain to you."

Taylor took her hand and pressed it to her cheek. "My parents were very honest with me." She released Jessie's hand and began to walk deeper among the mums and fall flowers. "They told me that you were very young - 15 or 16, I think - and weren't prepared for parenthood."

Jessie wasn't sure what she had expected, but it wasn't having the facts of her past laid out by her own daughter. She said nothing

."When I was 16" Taylor continued, "I thought about you and what it must have been like for you. About what I would do if I had gotten pregnant." She paused then continued in her soft voice. "I tried to imagine my life at 16 with a baby to take care of. I wouldn't know what to do, either. So" she stopped and faced Jessie again "what I'm trying to say is, I'm glad you decided to let me live and to have the wonderful life that I have. My parents are wonderful, I have a younger brother, and not for one moment have I thought or heard anything bad about you."

Tears were running down Jessie's cheeks as she listened to Taylor. They stared at each other for a moment, then Jessie spoke. "I hope we can be friends" she said, choking back a new onslaught of emotion. "I would never try to take the place of your parents, but... but I hope we can build on this and have a relationship we can both cherish."

Taylor rubbed her shoe along the ground, as though she would find the words she needed somewhere there. Jessie held her breath, not certain if she should expect an answer that would end their relationship before it began.

"What I'm not sure about" Taylor said in a soft voice, "is what I should call you." She looked into Jessie's face and saw a smile full of admiration.

"I think" Jessie exhaled with quiet relief "that Jessie will do just fine."

And that was it. The beginning of a friendship built from a fragile bond that had separated them years before, but had remained intact through Jessie's own mother. As they walked quietly back to the house, Jessie said a silent prayer of thanks to her mother for having kept her hope alive that this reunion would someday take place.

Nicole and Jessie walked through the mall, stopping at a small shop.

"Look", Jessie picked up a green cashmere sweater. "Wouldn't this look beautiful on Taylor?"

"Mmmmm," Nicole agreed. "Why don't you get it for her for Christmas?"

"Good idea," Jessie said as she checked the size. "But I might give it to her before then. It would be nice for her to wear around the Holidays."

"Fine. Go ahead and get it then, and let's go." Nicole's impatience caught Jessie by surprise. After all, she knew, shopping was up there on Nicole's list of favorite things to do. Right after bitching and throwing tantrums.

"What's with you?" Jessie said as they walked to the register.

"Nothing," Nicole said as she glanced at her watch. "We've been here for hours and I'd like to go home."

"Are you expecting someone?"

"Who would I be expecting?" Nicole sulked. It's not like I know anyone around here." She leaned closed to Jessie. "I'm not feeling too well, that's all."

"Oh" Jessie said, still puzzled by her sister's unusually anxious behavior. "Well then just let me pay for this and we'll go."

Once back at the house, Nicole stretched out on the sofa and closed her eyes. "I haven't heard from him in almost two weeks" she suddenly offered.

"From who?"

"From Matt" Nicole snapped. "He said he would call and he didn't."

"Then call him" Jessie said sensibly.

"I can't call him" Nicole countered. "It's not like that yet."

"Nicole" Jessie came and sat next to her sister. "We're not teenagers. If you want to talk to Matt, pick up the phone and call him."

"I think he has a wife."

Jessie couldn't contain her laughter. "Trust me" she patted Nicole's slender hand "Matt is not married, nor does he have another woman in his life."

"Did Jake tell you that?"

Jessie nodded. "Yes" she stated simply. "He also told me that Matt is crazy about you."

"Oh stop" Nicole said with a bit of hope in her voice. "I've only seen him a couple of times."

Jessie raised her eyebrows but held her tongue.

"Besides" Nicole groaned "I'm still not certain he's gotten past what a fool I made of myself on that damn canoe trip that mother made us take."

"Well, if you're not going to call him, then let's retire to the porch and open mother's last letter." Nicole sighed heavily but stood and walked toward the kitchen. "I'll mix up a good strong batch of Aunt Gert's martinis. God only knows what mother's grand finale will be."

Nicole walked from the kitchen with the pitcher of peach martinis and found Jessie loading the wood in the fireplace.

"Oh" Nicole said happily "a fire. What a great idea. Are we going to burn the last letter instead of reading it?"

"Afraid not, sis. It's just a bit too windy out there to enjoy a martini. I thought we'd get a little toasty with a fire."

"I'd rather get toasted with these martinis. I have a feeling we'll need it" she said as she poured the martinis and ripped open the envelope marked "Open after Thanksgiving"."

Thanksgiving Dinner with Andre Luc and Ben was lovely, wasn't it?"

"It was" Jessie agreed as she settled into the chair next to the fireplace. "Andre is such a fabulous cook. And Ben is so good for him. Kind of keeps him centered."

"Well, here goes" Nicole said and began to read aloud.

Happy Holidays, Darlings!

I imagine it has been quite a year for both of you and I hope you are not too terribly angry with me for all I've put you through. It was only with the greatest love in my heart that I wrote each word and made each request of you. It was also with a great deal of faith that I knew you would carry out each and every task I prepared for you.

So now we come to the end.

As I write this, my heart is heavy with longing to hold each of you, as I know you feel the same way. But I never lived my life holding on to sadness, and I don't want you to live that way either. So here is my final request of you.

I want you to host the best Christmas party that has ever

been hosted. It needn't be the biggest, but everything about it must be the best. The best decorations, the best food, the best music, and certainly the best of friends.

Hold me in your hearts, Darlings, as I have always held you both.

Love forever,

Mother

The sisters were quiet for a while, pondering the tender words and holding their mother in their hearts. Their thoughts went to the past months of "tasks" that had been assigned to them, feeling proud that they had followed her wishes. The times they didn't understand were becoming clearer each day now and as if on cue, they glanced at each other and smiled. They recognized each other as the sisters they had become and the women that they were. A solidarity had formed between them and both knew it was a unity that would not be broken by time or distance.

"Finally" Nicole said as she wiped a tear from her eye "something that doesn't require paddling, sweating, or searching for that damn inner goddess that obviously went AWOL."

Jessie laughed at her sister "And this is right up your alley, Nicole. Planning a party."

Nicole was suddenly breathless with excitement. "We'll have to call someone in the morning to come and decorate. We can't invite too many because this place isn't very big, and"

"Wait" Jessie suddenly interrupted "mother didn't say we had to have the party here. Why don't we have it at the ranch?"

"Oh" Nicole clapped her hands like a child "what a fabulous idea! I'm so excited I can't wait to start planning this. Who should we invite?"

Jessie was thrilled to see her sister's enthusiasm after this morning's mood, and found herself almost as excited as Nicole.

"Every year" she started "the staff at the ranch has made a big deal of decorating the house for me. It's been their gift to me, and it's become a tradition."

"Then we'll invite all of your staff. How many is that?"

"About 10, plus Jake."

Nicole gave Jessie a knowing glance. "Yes" she said smugly. "I wouldn't consider Jake 'staff' either."

"And we'll invite Matt" Jessie added, ignoring Nicole's remark. "And Aunt Gert will definitely add some life to the party."

"As long as she leaves her bowling balls at home" Nicole laughed. "What about Andre Luc and Ben? We can't leave them out. That's about 17 people, including you and me."

Jessie's excitement was nearly equal to Nicole's. "And Willie and Miss Violet? They're so dear. Do you think we could get Willie to leave the Island for a few hours?"

"I think Miss Violet could get him to go anywhere she wanted" Jessie smirked. "Willie absolutely adores her."

"And do you think Taylor will bring someone?" Nicole asked brightly.

"I guess that would be up to her, but I certainly hope so."

"So that's about 20 or 21 guests" Nicole said happily. "I think that's plenty. Now" she said, "when do you think we should have this soiree?"

Jessie went to the kitchen and returned studying the calendar. "Christmas is on a Monday. Do you think Saturday the 23rd?"

"I think that's great but it doesn't give us much time" Nicole worried. "Are we going to have a dinner?"

The sisters looked at each other contemplating the issue. "No" Nicole answered "let's just make it lots of hors d'oeuvres, wonderful Christmas music, oh" she jumped up "let's hire some carolers. Wouldn't that be divine?"

"I don't know about divine" Jessie teased "but it would be festive."

Nicole grabbed a pad and pen from the table and began to make notes. "Do you think the Mormon Tabernacle Choir is available?" she joked.

Jessie laughed and Nicole continued. "Okay, so should we just hire a DJ?"

Jessie shook her head "Too impersonal" she countered. "Let's just have some nice background music. I'd like the company and the conversation to keep the party lively, not some DJ blaring 'Jingle Bell Rock' throughout the house."

"Good idea" Nicole agreed. "So" she scribbled "we have to go out and buy every Christmas CD we can find."

"I have some CDs" Jessie offered and watched Nicole roll her eyes.

"What?" Jessie defended "I have some perfectly acceptable Christmas music."

"Is it Ernest Tubbs or Gene Autry" Nicole commented dryly.

"It's neither" Jessie sniffed. "You'll see. I love Christmas music and I buy some new ones every year."

"Okay" Nicole compromised "next time Jake comes by, we'll have him bring all of your Christmas music and I'll study your collection."

"Fine" Jessie agreed "but I think you'll be in for a pleasant surprise. By the way" she smiled dryly "who did you have in mind? Some heavy rockers from England?"

"Nooo." Nicole argued, "I don't even like heavy rock."

Jessie groaned but let the music subject drop. "What about food? Who do you think we should call?"

"Well, it can't be anyone from Pawley's Island" Nicole said. "I don't think they'd want to come all the way out to the ranch."

"Oh, I know" Jessie offered. "Miss Nell has a friend who does catering."

"Perfect" Nicole agreed. "Does she make something that's not fried?"

"Nicole" Jessie scolded. "Do you always have to be so sarcastic?"

"I was raised in England" Nicole answered. "It's what we do."

"Well, sometimes it's just too much" Jessie answered.

"And for that matter" Nicole retorted "do you always have to be so Southern?"

Jessie gave her sister a surprised look, but then both laughed.

"I guess our differences really do get in the way at times," Nicole offered. "I think the only thing we ever shared was mother's birth canal."

For the next hour the sisters laid out a menu of light to moderate food that could easily match the finest restaurants in Charleston and London.

"Well" Jessie yawned "I've about had it with party planning 101."

"Me too" Nicole agreed. "When can we go out to the ranch again to have a look around?"

"Well, I guess we can take a ride tomorrow" Jessie offered. "And if we're going to do that, I'm going to bed."

"Me, too" Nicole stood and stretched. "I have quite a large CD collection to review tomorrow" and gave her sister a devious grin.

They arrived at the ranch early and found Jake in the

kitchen talking to Miss Nell. When Jessie and Nicole walked in, Jake turned and gave Jessie a huge smile and walked to her side.

"Hey" he said as he put his arm around her shoulder. "Good to see you, Jess."

"You, too Jake" she said and slid her arm easily around his waist. "Show me how things are going with our guests from Florida" she said as they turned and walked toward the barn.

"Honestly" Miss Nell said as they watched from the window. "For the life of me I don't know what those two are waiting for."

Nicole laughed. "I agree. Cupid has so many arrows in their butts I'm surprised they can sit down."

Miss Nell howled with laughter. "Can I get you a cup of coffee, Miss Nicole?"

"Only if you join me," Nicole answered. "I'd like to talk to you about your friend's catering business."

As Jake and Jessie walked into the barn, Jake stopped and took her hand, turning her to face him.

"I've missed you, Jess" he said earnestly.

She averted her gaze and tried to sound less elated than she was at seeing him. "I've missed you too, Jake. I know I've put a lot on your shoulders this past year."

He lifted her chin and moved closer to her face as he whispered "That's not what I mean."

She stood rock still as Jake gently touched her lips with his. As he lifted his mouth from hers, he said softly "That's how I missed you."

"Jake" she said breathlessly "do you think this is a good idea?"

He smiled and slid his hand around her back "I think it's a great idea and" he tapped her chin with his finger "I think it's long past due."

"It's frightening to me." Jessie's voice was so soft he wasn't certain he'd heard her right.

Jake studied her somber expression and took her hands in his.

"Jess." He shook his head, gathering the words he wanted to get exactly right. "Are you frightened of me, or frightened of us?"

A slight smile started across her lips, but he stopped her with his words. "Because I think you know that there's nothing scary about me, so I can only assume you're afraid of us."

Jessie let him hold her hands but otherwise didn't respond. "You must know how I feel about you, and I'm pretty sure I know how you feel about me, so I don't get why we can't move ahead with a relationship."

"What if it doesn't....doesn't end the way you think it would?" Jessie's voice was soft, uncertain that her own words held any credibility.

Jake smiled and lifted her fingers to his lips. "I don't think it would end at all."

She looked into his face for the first time since their conversation had begun. She saw his honesty and the natural belief he held in his own words. Jake was so strong and good in so many ways and Jessie knew her line of reasoning was flawed. She was looking at the practical side and dismissing her own emotions. She could no longer deny that she had buried her feelings for Jake for too long, and the time was at hand to either take a chance or lose him forever.

"Can I think about it?" Jessie asked.

"No" Jake laughed quietly. "I'm pretty sure you've already thought about it so I'm asking you for a decision." Jake's eyes were smiling but his voice was steady and sure. "Jess? Can I have an answer? Can you and I start to build something together or is this where it begins and ends?"

Jessie's mind was in turmoil, but she knew that Jake was right. She had to give him an answer. She'd thought about it for months – maybe for years if she were to be honest – and now she realized that if she said no, Jake would likely leave the ranch.

The basic logic of her answer was so apparent to her now, that she had so smile.

Jake read her smile and her eyes and wrapped his arms around her, holding her tightly and whispered "If you're not in love with me now, Jess, I'm going to make sure that you fall in love with me everyday."

Jessie smiled as she held him, feeling the strength of his love pour over her.

"I don't think it'll take much" she whispered.

Jake shifted his head and looked into Jessie's eyes, then kissed her softly. "It may use up every ounce of strength I have, Jess, but we'll take things as slowly as you want. I promise."

They walked silently toward the stalls and Jake turned back to the business side of their relationship. "This is Casper" he said as he stroked the white horse's head. "He had a rough time in the beginning but he's as healthy and solid as they come now."

Jessie spoke softly to the horse for a few minutes, then Jake took her by the hand and showed her the other horses that had been brought to them as neglected and downtrodden and were now healthy and clear eyed.

"You've done a terrific job with them, Jake."

"It was mostly Brian and Sam that took on the lion's share of the work," Jake conceded.

"Well, I'll have to make sure I see them to tell them how grateful I am."

As they walked back to the house hand-in-hand, Jessie told Jake about their mother's final letter and the plans they had for the party. When they entered the kitchen, Nicole and Miss Nell were huddled over the notes that Nicole had brought along.

"Oh Jess" she exclaimed, "Miss Nell's friend Patsy is so excited about the party. I spoke to her on the phone and she has the most terrific ideas!"

"Really" Jess answered, never taking her eyes from Jake. "So the menu is all set?"

"All set" Nicole announced proudly, then suddenly caught the look between Jake and Jessie. "Um, I think I'll go look at your famous CD collection" she said as she stepped backwards from the room. She suddenly felt like she was in the middle of a party that she hadn't been invited to. "Nell" she said "would you mind showing me where Jessie keeps them?"

Alone in the kitchen, Jake walked toward the door, stopping in front of where Jessie stood at the counter. "Why don't we go out and get some lunch" he said.

Jessie nodded, jolted by the electricity that Jake was sending through her. "About noon?" she asked, trying to sound nonchalant.

Nicole and Miss Nell removed their ears from the other side of the door and gave each other a congratulatory hug.

"It's about time" Nicole whispered.

"Do you think we should plan a wedding instead of Christmas party?" Nell giggled.

On the ride home the next morning, Jessie was especially tight-lipped about her and Jake, despite Nicole's unending questions.

"Well, what did he say?" Nicole asked for the fifth time.

"Nicole" Jessie said patiently "can we please talk about the party? We need to get the invitations out as soon as possible."

"Oh screw the invitations" she pouted. "We'll just call everyone. Now tell me what Jake said or I think I'll explode."

Jessie suddenly pulled the car to the side of the road and turned in her seat to face her sister.

"What he said, Nicole," she started patiently, "is that he thinks - and has always thought - that we belong together and if it takes him the rest of his life, he'll convince me of the same thing."

Nicole sat wide-eyed and stunned, unable to speak at first. The sisters stared at each other until Jessie moved to put the car back in gear. Nicole's hand stopped her motion and Jessie looked over at Nicole.

"Wow" was all Nicole could manage at first, but soon collected herself. "Please tell me you didn't turn him down?"

"I didn't turn him down" Jessie said.

"Thank God" Nicole almost shouted. "This guy is in love with you, Jessie."

"It's complicated, Nicole."

"No, Jessie, it's not" she countered quickly. "Politics are complicated - shit, looking for our inner goddess is complicated. Jake being in love with you is not complicated."

"Don't push me, Nicole. Jake and I will work things out. And" she eyed Nicole seriously "I don't want to talk about it anymore."

Nicole assumed her usual position, arms crossed, mouth set in a stern pout, but said nothing more about the issue.

"The menu is planned?" Jessie asked after a few miles of icy silence from Nicole.

"Done" Nicole answered. "And I must say I was quite surprised by your CD collection."

"Told you" Jessie teased.

"No cowboys, no choirs, but I did find that one Perry Como CD" Nicole joked.

Jessie put her hand up toward Nicole "No lie, Nicole, that was mother's favorite."

"Sure it was" Nicole teased and laughed. "So how did it wind up in your CD collection at the ranch?"

"Okay, okay" Jessie conceded, "so maybe I am a bit partial to the old crooner."

The sisters talked the rest of the way back to Pawley's Island about the party and by the time they stopped in their Grandmother's driveway, the details were set and they had decided to spend the next day shopping for their party clothes.

A few days before the party, Jessie was in the kitchen making breakfast when she heard a terrible commotion and turned in time to see Nicole tumbling down the stairs.

"Oh my God, Nicole" she screamed and ran to her sister who was lying in a heap at the bottom the stairway. "Are you hurt?" she cried.

Nicole was staring up at her sister, unblinking and in obvious pain. "My ankle" she said tearfully. "I think it's broken."

Jessie helped Nicole sit up, then dialed 9-1-1. Within minutes the emergency crew was inside checking Nicole's leg and foot. "I'm not sure if it's broken" the older paramedic said to the sisters, "but it looks like a pretty bad sprain at the least."

"Oh God" Nicole pleaded "what about the party?"

Jessie and the paramedic tried to calm Nicole, explaining that a sprained ankle was nothing like an amputation and that she would do just fine for the party on crutches.

"Crutches!" she howled. "I'll be wearing Gucci and hobbling around on aluminum legs?"

The medic was at first confused and then amused by Nicole's dramatic reception to the news that she would, indeed, have to go in the ambulance to the hospital for X-rays and treatment. But once inside the vehicle, with no audience present, Nicole settled into a quiet, self-pitying sob.

The morning routine at the hospital made Nicole even more nervous, and when Jessie finally arrived Nicole was in a complete panic.

"What's going to happen to me?" Nicole pleaded.

"Calm down, Nicole. They're going to take X-rays of your ankle and your foot to make sure it's not broken, they'll give you some pain medication, wrap your ankle and send you home with me."

Tears began to slide from Nicole's eyes. "It does hurt terribly, Jess," she said in a small voice.

Jessie took her sister's hand to comfort her. "I know" she said softly "but they'll be taking you for X-rays in a few minutes and we'll be out of here in no time."

True to her word, in just a few hours Jessie was helping Nicole out of the car and into the house. Slightly woozy from the pain medication, Nicole wobbled on the crutches and Jessie steadied her and led her toward the sofa.

"Get some rest," she instructed Nicole "and I'll fix us something to eat. Are you hungry?"

"No" Nicole giggled "just thirsty. Is it too early for a martini?"

Jessie rolled her eyes and said "I don't think a martini and a percocet would go too well together, Nicole." Before another minute had passed, Nicole's eyes were closed and she slid into a peaceful slumber.

Jessie went to the kitchen and dialed Jake's cell. She told him about Nicole's tumble and the visit to the emergency room.

"No" she answered him "it's not broken but it's a pretty bad sprain. I'm afraid she won't be wearing those new shoes she bought for the party," she laughed.

"Jess" Jake said insistently "Matt came in last night. Why don't we come over for a few days and give you a hand. I have a feeling your sister is going to be a handful until she learns how to navigate on crutches."

"Oh, Jake, that would be great, but don't you and Matt have plans?"

"Not really" Jake lied. "Besides, I think Matt is kind of anxious to see Nicole again."

"Really?" Jessie said.

"And I'm kind of anxious to see you too, Jess."

She smiled "Me, too."

"Good" Jake said confidently "see you tonight."

When Nicole awoke later that afternoon, her mood was foul.

"Are you out of your mind?" she chastised Jessie. "Matt is coming here to see me teetering around on crutches?"

"Oh Nicole" Jessie humored her sister "just think of him as your knight in shining armor coming to rescue you."

"I'm hardly a damsel in distress" Nicole snapped.

Jessie glanced from her sister's face to her ankle, wrapped in a bulky bandage. "Oh I'd say you are most definitely in distress."

"Piss off," Nicole said sharply. "This hurts and I hardly think it's fair that you're making fun of me."

"Here," Jessie handed her sister a small pill. "It's time to take another one of these."

"Is that for the pain?" Nicole asked.

"No" Jessie smiled sweetly "it's for the attitude."

Jake and Matt arrived a little after 5:00 carrying 2 large

pizza boxes.

"Did you eat yet?" Jake called as they came through the door.

"Not yet" Jessie answered as she took the food from Jake and greeted Matt.

"How's the patient?" Matt asked as he walked over to where Nicole sat with her leg propped up on the ottoman.

"Miserable" she said, tears in her eyes. "This is going to be a terrible Christmas" she began to cry.

"Oh c'mon" Matt said as he sat next to her and kissed her damp cheek. "It won't be so bad. Just think of all the people that will wait on you."

"But I'm the hostess" she said tearfully. "What kind of a hostess can I be like this?" she pointed to her ankle.

"The kind that sits in her chair looking absolutely beautiful and acting as gracious as ever" Matt coaxed her.

She glanced over at Matt and smiled for the first time that day. "Matt" she said sweetly "you're probably just what I needed."

"Of course I am, honey," he laughed. "And more than that, you're just what I needed."

Nicole laid her head on his shoulder and they talked and ate pizza and laughed with Jake and Jessie.

"So, what are the sleeping arrangements?" Jake asked. "Do I have my choice of bedrooms?" he asked with a devilish grin.

"Sure you do" Jessie teased. "You can have the other sofa down here or the spare room upstairs."

"Wait a minute" Matt protested laughing. "I think I need to stay down here with Nicole."

"Actually" Nicole chimed in "I think that would be pretty safe."

"I don't think safety is what he has in mind, Nicole" Jessie laughed.

In the end, Matt decided to sleep on the other sofa so he could be close to Nicole if she needed him during the night. Jake opted for the spare room upstairs and as he walked Jessie up the stairs, he gave her a gentle nudge.

"Last chance" he teased. She kissed his cheek and smiled. Jake groaned but headed for the room he'd been assigned.

"Jake," Jessie glanced over her shoulder. "Just so you know, my door doesn't have a lock on it" and she slipped into her room.

The next morning when Jessie went to check on Nicole she found her standing in her closet, leaning against the wall and crying.

"Hey sis," she wrapped her arm around her sister. "What's going on with you? Are you in pain? Let me get you another pill."

"I don't need another pill. I've been up all night, Jessie." Nicole wiped her eyes.

"Did you and Matt have a fight?" Jessie asked, concerned about her sister's obvious distress.

"No, no, no, nothing like that. He's really great, you know."

"And he's crazy about you, sweetie. So what's the long face for?"

"He needs to find someone else to take to the party. Look at me. I look like an old lady on these crutches. I was going to wear a new Armani dress I had shipped in from London last week with these absolutely to die for shoes. But you know what Jess? It doesn't matter what I wear. The only thing anyone is going to see are these stupid old lady crutches. Hell, I might as well show up in my bathrobe with curlers in my hair."

"I don't think it matters to Matt what you wear" Jessie offered.

"It matters to me" Nicole sobbed.

"I know it does, but we'll figure something out. Why don't you go for a long soak in the tub and we'll talk about it later."

"You're such a good sister." Nicole wrapped her arm around Jessie and they hobbled into the bathroom.

"You're a good sister, too. Stoned but good."

"Those are really good pills that Doctor gave me, Jess. I don't feel a thing."

"Really, I hadn't noticed."

With Nicole soaking in the tub, Jessie busied herself in Nicole's closet looking through the massive amounts of designer cloths that hung there, some still with the tags on."

"You sure have a lot of dresses" Jessie yelled into the bathroom.

"That's one of the perks of being a personal shopper. All the design houses want me to use their fashions so they send me all kinds of free stuff. If you see something you like, try it on."

"What's this one in the hanging bag? This is beautiful

Nicole. Why don't you wear this?"

"That's my funeral dress, but if you want to wear it to the holiday party, go for it."

Jessie walked into the bathroom carrying the dress in the bag. "Your funeral dress? What are you talking about? Like a dress you'd wear to a funeral, right?"

"No silly, it's for when I die. Go ahead, open the bag. There's a note inside with instructions."

Jessie slowly unzipped the bag and pulled out a white envelope with her name written on it. "Oh great. Another white envelope. When were you going to tell me about this, Nicole? Or was I just supposed to find it after you're dead. And how do you know that I'll still be alive when you die?"

"50-50 shot. Those are good odds, don't you think?" Bubbles surrounded Nicole, her bandaged leg hanging out of the tub.

Jessie opened the envelope began to read.

Things to do for my funeral:

- *Make sure that I have had a manicure and a pedicure. I prefer L'Oreal's toasted bronze but if you can't find that, Sunsets in Bermuda by*

Maybelline is fine.

- *I want peach martinis served after my funeral and I have a case of martini glasses set aside so everyone can take one home as a memento of the occasion.*

"You want me to give gifts out at your funeral?" Jessie continued to read.

"Just something small and tasteful" Nicole said. "In the box I have some CD's of music that I would like played. Please only use my music, I don't want any of that country twangy shit. And I would like for George Clooney to read my eulogy" Nicole added off-handedly.

"What if George can't make it, Nicole?" Jessie was amused by her sister and the entire discovery of her funeral plans added a new dimension to Nicole's planning abilities.

"I have a list of substitutes."

"Of course you do."

"I have also enclosed some photos so that you can have my makeup done by a professional."

"You want some orange saucer lips?" Jessie laughed.

"I will haunt you for the rest of your life if you even think about it."

"No orange saucer lips. Got it."

Nicole continued as though she were ordering a cake for a party. "I want to have a spray tan, but not so dark that it looks fake. Just a little color so I don't look so washed out."

"You'll be dead, Nicole, but I get it. No fake tan. Is that it? Or does your highness have any other request that I should be made aware of?"

"One last thing, but I think I forgot to put it on the list" Nicole said as she swooped up a handful of bubble and blew them playfully toward Jessie.

"What's that Nicole?"

"I only want white flowers at my funeral. No pink carnations or red roses. If anyone sends them, just have them shipped to the hospital."

"That it?"

"I think so, but if I think of anything else, I'll just add it to the list. You know Jess, I could help you pick out your funeral clothes if you want" Nicole offered sincerely.

"Yeah, sure Nicole, we'll get right on that" Jessie said as she zipped the bag and replaced it in the closet. "I think you need to get out of the tub now. I'm pretty sure the hot water is screwing up your head."

"So you don't care what happens at your funeral?" Nicole asked as she hobbled to the bed.

"Not in the least. I don't care what I wear, I don't care if there are pink or red flowers and frankly I don't care who gives my eulogy."

Nicole looked at Jessie squarely. "Are you sure we're sisters?"

"I've been asking myself that same question for the last year. You rest now and I'll put some ice packs on your ankle."

"OK," Nicole mumbled as she closed her eyes. "Tell Matt, I'm sorry about spraining my ankle and that I look like an old . . . "

Jessie pulled the blanket up, shut off the lights and closed the door. An hour later Nicole made her way into the kitchen where Jessie, Jake and Matt were eating lunch.

"Are you feeling better?" Jessie asked as she slid her arm under Nicole's and helped her to the chair.

"Much better, thanks," she replied, "but I can't find my crutches."

Matt walked out on the deck and returned with the

crutches. "We fixed them up a bit for you. Do you like them?"

The crutches had been painted shiny black and the arm cushions had been covered with black and white striped fabric. A few rhinestones had been glued down the front, so they sparkled when the light hit them.

"Go ahead," Matt said. "Give them a whirl."

"You did this for me?" Nicole asked as tears welled up in her eyes. "I don't know what to say."

Matt put his hand gently on Nicole's chin. "Say you'll go to the party."

"Well, I certainly can't turn down an offer like that" Nicole said as she tried out her new crutches. "These are great. I think there might be a market for designer crutches. My clients in London would love these."

A few days before the party, they all headed back to the ranch. Nicole was feeling better and was actually managing quite well with her new crutches. Unless, of course, Matt was close by. Then she became quite helpless.

Matt saw right through her act, but didn't mind. It was all part of Nicole's charm as far as he was concerned.

The house was completely decorated and it looked like a wonderland. As the evening fell, the lights in the trees looked like thousands of tiny stars dancing in the breeze. The garland hung from the eaves and the lights were wound through the green wreaths that were adorned with huge red bows and hung in every window. There were festive trees in each room, decorated with every bright Christmas color.

The kitchen was buzzing with activity already. Patsy the caterer had an extra refrigerator brought in to hold all of the delicacies she was still preparing. The aroma of cider and apples mixed with the delicate scent of warm bread and pastries.

"Wow" Jessie said as she came into the kitchen. "This is all for one party?"

"Well" Nell said "it's not just any party, Miss Jessica. This is a celebration of quite a year for you and your sister."

"Yes it is" Jessie said happily. "Quite a year indeed."

"How is Miss Nicole getting on?" Nell asked.

"I'm ready to dance" Nicole called as she entered the kitchen on her crutches.

"Look at you" Nell exclaimed. "Where did you find black sequined crutches?"

"It's all about presentation" Nicole joked. "I think they're going to look fabulous with my Armani dress," Nicole laughed. "Besides, I can guarantee there will be no one else at the party with sequined crutches."

Everything was checked by Nicole and Jessie and as the evening wound down, Nicole was the first to retire. Matt made a show of sweeping her off her crutches and carrying her up the stairs to her room. No one missed the fact that Matt didn't re-appear for the rest of the night.

As the guests arrived on Saturday evening, Jessie and Nicole were both in high spirits. Everything came off beautifully, but when Taylor arrived, Jessie was nervous about introducing her to everyone. She had told Jake about Taylor but she wasn't certain how many of her other friends had gotten word that Jessie had a grown daughter. Nicole hooked her arm through Taylor's and hung onto both her crutches and Taylor.

"Everyone" she clamored for attention "I'd like you all to meet my wonderful niece, Jessie's daughter Taylor."

Andre Luc and Ben swept over to Taylor and began to pepper her with compliments and questions.

Brian took one look at Taylor and fell in love. Sam reminded him that this was the boss's daughter, but Brian couldn't take his eyes off of Taylor. And once Taylor noticed Brian, the two became inseparable for the rest of the evening.

"Isn't she just the one to take the edge off for me?" Jessie whispered to Jake.

Jake put his arm around Jessie's shoulder. "I told you there was nothing to worry about. I mean look at her." He motioned toward where Taylor stood talking to Brian. "She's almost as beautiful as her mother." Jessie laughed and gave Jake a nudge in the ribs.

Aunt Gert had been the last to arrive with a short balding man that Jessie and Nicole assumed to be her latest boyfriend. Aunt Gert gushed as she introduced him around the party. When she came to Nicole and Matt, Gert motioned for Jessie and Jake to join them.

"I'd like you to meet Ernie" she said proudly. "And you can now refer to me as Mrs. Edmonds."

The foursome raised eyebrows and Nicole and Jessie hugged Aunt Gert.

"You got married?" Jessie had a hard time picturing her headstrong Aunt with this little mouse of a man.

"Aunt Gert" Nicole cajoled "you sly devil. Keeping this a secret from us. When did you get married?"

Ernie the mouse blushed slightly as Gert slipped her arm through his. "We just flew out to Las Vegas and got married in one of those little wedding chapels." She winked at Jake. "Our best man was an Elvis impersonator."

"You don't say" Jake answered, not certain if she was serious. "Who was your maid of honor," he said sincerely "Marilyn Monroe?"

Gert laughed and Ernie blushed again, but Jake was still struggling with the mental picture of Gert, Ernie and Elvis.

The party was all that Jessie and Nicole hoped it would be and the evening slipped by much too quickly. As the last few guests left, Jessie stood with Jake on the porch watching the lights in the trees as they swayed in the breeze.

"It was a great party, Jess."

"It was, wasn't it?" she answered as she felt the warmth of Jake's arm around her shoulder. "I think Taylor and Brian are about to become the next big item" she added.

"Well" Jake answered "they make a pretty good couple. They actually seemed like a perfect fit right from the start."

Jessie looked into Jake's face. "Kind of like someone else we know?"

Jake bent to give Jessie a gentle kiss. "Kind of" he smiled.

"Hmm" she said as she turned toward the door. "I think we'd better go chaperone my sister and Matt. Those two have been on fire since we got here."

"I've noticed" Jake said as he opened the door. "And by the way, what did Nicole mean when she said her inner goddess had finally shown up?"

CHAPTER 15
COMMITMENT ISSUES

Matt and Jake split their time between the ranch and Pawley's Island for the next few weeks. If they weren't with Nicole and Jessie on the island, then the sisters were at the ranch.

When Matt finally announced that he had to leave for Florida in a few more days, Jessie was certain there would be hell to pay with Nicole's foul mood until he returned.

Jessie smiled as she heard Nicole maneuver herself down the stairs, waiting for the sound of her sister cursing the crutches and the entire house. As Nicole rounded the corner she was smiling and greeted her sister with a cheery "Good Morning!"

"Have you hit that bottle of happy pills again? I thought the pain was gone and you didn't need them anymore."

Nicole laughed, "I don't need them anymore" she countered. "It's a wonderful new year and I'm just on a natural high at the thought of moving back here and spending more time with you."

Jessie placed her cup on the table. She studied Nicole's face for a hint that what she had just said was a joke.

"What?" Nicole said. "Didn't I tell you that I have decided

to move back to the States?"

"I think I would have remembered that bit of information" Jessie responded as she slid into her chair.

"Oops."

"Big oops" Jessie countered. "So when did you make this decision? And why?"

Nicole placed her hand over Jessie's and her tone became serious. "You have become my best friend" she started "and I don't want to lose you. I don't want to go through another year wondering what you're doing and how your life is coming along." She took a deep breath and continued. "My life in London is lovely...but it just doesn't mean that much to me anymore. It took having you in my life this past year to make me realize that."

Jessie had been feeling the same way as the end of their time together came close, but she didn't feel she had the right to ask her sister to give up her life and career and move to South Carolina.

Tears welled up and Jessie had to swallow hard to find her voice. "Nicole, I'm so happy you'll be coming here. I didn't want you to leave, but thought asking you to stay would be too selfish."

They locked their fingers tightly and let the tears slide

down their cheeks, sniffling and laughing at each other.

"Well" Nicole said as she brushed her tears aside "we have a lot to talk about and a lot of decisions to make, don't we?" She started to move her hand, but Jessie held it tightly. Nicole looked at her sister.

"What?"

"Matt" Jessie said. "What about Matt?"

Nicole took a deep breath and wiped her cheeks until they were finally dry. "Matt is actually the one that put the idea in my head. We had a wonderful chat and he asked me some questions that forced me to think about my life."

Jessie nodded and let her sister continue at her own pace.

"Matt made me realize that while shopping for women who are filthy with money and ego is undoubtedly a blessed profession," she smiled, "it doesn't compare to primping up a thrift store or bathing a grimy horse. And" she smiled at Jessie "it doesn't even come close to having my family."

Jessie smiled and coaxed an answer out of Nicole. "What about you and Matt? Are you going to move to Florida?"

Nicole gave Jessie an incredulous look. "There are alligators in Florida" she sniffed "so I most certainly will not be moving there."

"So?" Jessie pressed.

"So Matt will be moving here" Nicole said, as if the answer should have been obvious to her sister.

Jessie took the next few words cautiously. "So you and Matt...are staying together?"

Nicole shrugged. "Another product of our little chats. Seems you and I aren't the only ones that would like to resolve our commitment issues."

Jessie started to object, but held her tongue.

"I'll get a place of my own here and when Matt is able to make the move – he has to sell his businesses and all – we'll see how we get on living together."

Jessie cocked her head back and smiled. "Wow" she blinked. "That's quite a move for both of you."

Nicole shrugged. "And so what about you and Jake? Will you finally let him move into 'the big house'?" she teased.

Jessie grew quiet for a moment, then shook her head. "It's not as simple as all that."

"Oh" Nicole mocked, "moving from London, moving from

Florida, selling businesses…I'd hardly say that's simple, Jess."

"That's not what I meant" she defended.

"Are you still hung up on this 'what-if-it-doesn't-work' thing because I have to tell you, that's gotten quite lame."

Jessie went for a fresh cup of coffee, prepared for Nicole to launch herself into another tirade.

Jessie cut her off. "It's just that Jake and I are going to take things a little slower."

"Oh. my. God" Nicole started. "He has been working for you for six years. If you take it any slower you'll both be trying to figure out how to hold hands while you maneuver your walkers."

Jessie had to laugh as she sat back down and sipped her coffee.

"This isn't the 19th century, Jess. Jake is a good looking man, he's smart and funny and he can have any woman he wants." Nicole reached across the table. "And he wants you."

Jessie looked up at her sister. "You think I have a commitment issue?"

Nicole's mouth fell open as she stared at her sister. "Ya think?" she answered and they both started laughing.

As the irony of Jess's question sunk in, their laughter turned to howling and neither could control themselves.

After a few minutes, Jessie shook her head. "I guess I need to look a little deeper if I'm going to figure this one out on my own."

"There's nothing to figure out" Nicole had suddenly slipped into the big sister role. "It's the oldest story in the book of love. You're afraid of getting hurt. Hell" she smirked "we all are. But guys like Jake and Matt don't come along everyday."

"So you think these are the two that we've been holding out for?" Jessie sipped her coffee.

"I'm just sayin...." Nicole laughed as she nodded. "These two could be the keepers."

Jessie nodded, letting her sister's words take hold then glancing at the clock.

"Well, those two 'keepers' want to meet us at Rusty's for lunch, so we'd better get ready. Matt's leaving in a few days so I'm sure you want to spend as much time as you can with him. "

As Jessie and Nicole entered Rusty's they found Jake and Matt seated in a corner booth. The men exchanged a strange look and stood as the sisters came to the table.

"What have you two been up to?" Nicole asked.

Jake and Matt both smiled but said nothing. Jake kissed Jessie on the cheek as he pulled her closer and Jessie got the distinct impression that something had transpired between the men that neither of the women were privy to.

A waitress appeared and took their drink orders then Matt picked the subject matter.

"So" he turned to face Nicole "did you have any news for your sister?"

Jessie's eyes widened "I'll say she did. Aren't you two just the epitome of discretion. Both of you moving to South Carolina, and setting up housekeeping together? Yeah" Jessie chuckled "I'd say she had some news for me."

Once again, Matt and Jake exchanged glances and the look wasn't missed by either of the sisters.

"Okay" Nicole said as the waitress reappeared with their drinks, "you two have obviously been up to something so you might as well spill it."

"Matt and I have decided that we needed to make some plans" Jake offered. "The two of you are wonderful, but you move at a snail's pace so we've had to take matters into our own hands."

This time it was Jessie and Nicole that exchanged a worried glance.

"What kind of plans?" Jessie asked.

Both Matt and Jake took a deep, collective breath then Matt cleared his throat to speak.

"We think we should have a double wedding" he said. Nicole's head very nearly snapped as she spun to look at Matt, and Jess's eyes widened toward Jake.

"What....what are you saying?" Jessie said.

"Well" Jake offered "that's when two couples get married at the same ceremony."

"You twit" Nicole finally laughed. "We know what a double wedding is. But..."

Jake finally took Jessie's hand and Matt did the same. "We're asking you girls to marry us." Jake looked into Jessie's eyes.

Matt turned to Nicole and placed a small kiss on her lips. "We think it's an idea whose time has come. What do you say?"

Jessie and Nicole were speechless, not realizing they were making it impossible for either of the men to breath. Jessie couldn't take her eyes from Jake and Nicole suddenly threw her arms around Matt's neck.

"Yes...yes...yes" she said as she sprinkled kisses on Matt's neck and cheeks.

Jake gazed at Jessie. "Well? You don't want to be the one to ruin a double wedding, do you?"

Jessie's mind was spinning like a tornado but as her eyes stayed locked with Jake's she found herself saying "I wouldn't dare ruin such a wonderful idea."

Jake slid his arm around her shoulder and pulled her to him, kissing her mouth as he whispered "I love you, Jess."

"I love you too" she smiled as his lips covered hers.

Nicole started crying then and Matt pulled her closer. "I hope those are the proverbial tears of joy." Nicole nodded as she dabbed at her eyes.

Jake motioned for the server and Rusty appeared at the table carrying a silver tray with four champagne glasses and asked if the time was right.

"Sure is" Jake beamed. Rusty placed the tray on the table

and gave Jake and Matt a wink. Matt quickly studied the glasses and picked one, handed it to Jake, and selected the other one. Tied to the glasses with a pink ribbon were diamond rings that each of the men untied and slipped onto the delicate fingers of the women who had just agreed to marry them.

"Jake" Jessie breathed. "This is beautiful."

"Matt" Nicole was crying openly now. "I've never been so happy."

"Well" Matt smiled "I hope you're happy because of me and not because that diamond weighs as much as a ship's anchor."

The waitress came back and poured the champagne, not wanting to intrude but unable to ignore the happiness that was flowing from the table.

"On the house" she smiled and settled the bottle into the ice. "Congratulations."

The couples toasted each other and spent the better part of the afternoon exchanging thoughts, enjoying a celebratory lunch, and agreeing that despite the tasks their mother had left for them, this turned out to be the best year any of them had ever had.

Jake drove with Jessie back to the house when Matt and

Nicole decided to spend some time window-shopping in Charleston since the day was unusually warm and sunny.

"Jess" Jake's voice was timid as he spoke. "I know we said we'd take it slow, but it seems like this is where we were both headed and face it, we're not teenagers. I love you and I don't see why we shouldn't have a real life together."

Jessie smiled as he said the words she now knew she had wanted to hear for so long.

"I love you too, Jake," knowing Jake was waiting for more. "I have to say, I didn't see a marriage proposal coming. At least not today. And when you put it that way, I agree. I suppose this is where we were headed eventually. It's not like we just met; we've known each other a long time. Maybe not as lovers, but as people. And I think that's more important, don't you?"

Jake squeezed her hand and Jessie moved closer to him. "So you're happy?" he smiled as he asked the question.

Jessie nudged him with her shoulder. "Of course I'm happy. I'm more than happy. I'm....I'm amazingly happy" she laughed.

"Up for some planning?" Jake asked. Jessie looked at his face, surprised at how open Jake was now that they had taken a step she thought was far in the future.

"You mean wedding planning?"

"No" he said as he shook his head. "I'll leave that up to you and Nicole. I'm talking about planning for the next few weeks, few months...and I guess for our life."

Jessie quieted for a moment, then sat up straighter. "I guess you should move into the house at the ranch."

Jake smiled at the thought. "When will you be moving back there? I mean, you and Nicole have taken care of all of your Mother's final wishes, haven't you?"

"Yes" Jessie sighed as she thought about the idea of not having another envelope waiting for her. "We'll meet with Mr. Justice tomorrow to settle the estate. And" she poked Jake in the ribs, "you two had better not be marrying us for our money."

"Just how much money are we talking about" Jake teased. "I mean, I could settle into a life of traveling around the world and eating at 5-star restaurants."

Jessie turned serious as she studied Jake's face. "You don't know how much money I'm about to inherit?"

Jake's brow furrowed. "How would I know that? I assumed it was enough to convince you and Nicole to go through all of the antics your Mother had you do this past year, but I never heard a dollar figure. And, Jess" he paused as he pulled into the driveway. "You don't need to tell me. Money has nothing to do with you and me."

"It's a lot," she offered quietly. "I mean, a really, really lot of money, Jake." Jake watched the expression on Jessie's face as she lowered her eyes and swallowed hard. "It's more money than we ever imagined my mother had. Its....we're talking....millions."

Jake thought for a moment that he was glad the car was parked because he surely would have run off the road at Jessie's admission. The silence filled the car like a balloon being inflated. It was the first time Jessie had told anyone about her inheritance, and saying the words aloud seemed to shock Jessie.

Jake cleared his throat and turned Jessie in her seat to face him. "Jess" he said, trying to grasp the fact that his new fiancé was about to inherit millions...plural. "That is your money, no matter how much it is. I don't want any part of it. Not now, not after we're married."

Jessie nodded as she took in his words. "I can't wrap my head around it yet" she said, her words the only sound in the car. "When we found out about our mother's will, we had no idea she had started another life, much less with a multi-millionaire." She glanced at Jake as she continued. "It's all just starting to hit me. Everything. Today is one of those days where everything is about to change. I'm going to get married" she smiled and squeezed Jake's hand. "I'm going to be a millionaire...there's so much I have to plan...we have to plan."

Jake and Jessie walked to the deck and sat for a few moments, the only sound coming from the gentle surf and the crowing of the gulls. Jake looked out at the ocean.

He studied Jessie for a moment, then spoke softly. "With that much money, Jess, you can have a life you've always dreamed of. Are you sure this is the one you want? With me?"

Jessie's eyes moved to his face, studying his strong features, which were now full of genuine uncertainty. She gave Jake a playful smile and said "If I didn't think I wanted you in my life, I'd have fired your ass years ago." She moved into his arms, nuzzling his neck. "It took six years" she said "and you finally made the biggest move of your life on me."

Jake's eyes widened as he held her away from him. "Are you serious? You're the one that always moved away from me."

"Well as my dear sister would say, you just don't know anything about women, do you, Jake?" she laughed.

The following weeks were filled with planning Nicole's move to the states, and after their meeting with Mr. Justice there were financial planners to meet. Jessie and Nicole felt like they had signed so many papers and documents they were certain there couldn't be anything left for them to sign.

Jessie and Nicole shared a rare, quiet evening on the deck, bundled against the gusty March wind.

"We haven't even had time to set our wedding date" Nicole said as she poured them each a martini. "I've done nothing but discuss money and sign papers. I'm certain" she said "that at one point I signed away any rights I may have had to Buckingham Palace."

Jessie laughed and sipped her drink. "Since you're not British I doubt that would have been an option for you."

"Have you spoken to Taylor lately?"

"Mmm hmm" Jessie nodded. "She and Brian are still an item."

"Is she happy for you and Jake?"

"Ecstatic" Jessie smiled as she leaned closer to her sister. "She's thrilled about all of it. The weddings, Brian, her new job...I get the feeling her and Brian are moving a lot more quickly than Jake and I did."

"A three-toed sloth moves faster than you and Jake did." All of the business obligations and the hectic pace of the past few weeks had not diminished Nicole's sense of humor. Jessie opted to let the remark move past her and she continued talking about Taylor.

"She's thinking about going back for her Masters in August."

"And what would she master?"

"Her interest must be genetic. Her degree is in Animal Science. I'm really proud of her."

"So her and Brian have a lot in common – being animal lovers and all."

"Taylor would like to become a vet. She told me Brian is all over her about getting her Masters as soon as possible."

Nicole's attention seemed to drift from the conversation and she sipped her drink, staring at the ocean.

After a few minutes, Nicole turned to Jessie. "Are you going to keep the ranch?"

Jessie cocked her head. "Of course we are. Why?"

"Would you sell Matt and me some of your acres so we could build a house out there?" The question came from Nicole as though she were asking to borrow a handbag or a scarf.

"I....I hadn't thought about it, but I guess I can talk to Jake. I have over 50 acres. How much land are you talking about?"

"Just a couple of acres - enough for a lovely house and a nice yard. It's not like I want to raise horses...I may get a puppy but nothing bigger than that. And I'd pay you a fair price, you know."

Jessie couldn't hide her surprise. "So we would be neighbors? Nicole! That would be so much fun. We could" Nicole held up her hand and cut Jessie off with a laugh.

"Don't think you're going to be popping over every morning for breakfast. Afternoon tea and biscuits, perhaps....but no breakfast."

"I wouldn't dream of coming by for breakfast. I've seen enough of you in the morning this past year to last me quite a few lifetimes."

Nicole looked at Jessie out of the corner of her eye. "So you'll do it? You'll sell Matt and me some of your land?"

"I said" Jessie poked Nicole's arm "I would speak to my future husband." She smiled and caught Nicole's eye as she added "I really don't think he'll have any objections."

Nicole jumped up and hugged her sister. "I can't wait" she turned toward the house. "I'm going to call Matt right now. We've talked about this so much and..." she stopped abruptly. "I'm doing it again, aren't I? Getting ahead of myself and setting myself up to be disappointed? Isn't that what you and Jake told me I do?"

"Yes it is" Jessie said. "Why don't you let me call Jake before you call Matt? But I want you to understand what this means." Jessie knew she had Nicole's attention and couldn't pass up the opportunity to snatch the wind from her sails – if only for a split second.

Nicole turned to Jessie, waiting for a list of restrictions on the real estate deal, but Jessie only winked and smiled as she said "More papers to sign."

As the weeks rolled into months, Nicole flew between London and Pawley's Island, bidding her friends farewell, shopping at Harrods and packing her new purchases to be shipped to the states. Jessie had to remind her that she could shop at Harrods anytime and she really should set some priorities for herself.

Jake moved into Jessie's house after he had announced to his crew the happy news that he and Jess had decided to get married. All of the men were thrilled and the only surprise among them was that it had taken six years.

It didn't take Matt long to close the transaction on his Florida dealerships. They had become well known and successful under Matt's business expertise and buyers were lined up as soon as word hit the street that they were for sale.

The plan was for Matt and Nicole to settle into the house on Pawley's Island but they split their time between Pawley's and Jessie's house. Construction on the home on their newly purchased property was under constant scrutiny by Matt, and Nicole began to understand why his business had been so successful. He paid attention to every detail, dealt with the workers fairly and with respect, and in return the construction crew worked tirelessly for his approval. He also reminded the crew that they really didn't want to deal with Nicole, which was the alternative to dealing with him.

Matt and Nicole approached Jake and Jess about holding off on the wedding until their house was completed and they had moved in. Since Jessie had agreed to take in several horses for training, they readily agreed, needing the extra time themselves.

"October would be a wonderful time for a wedding" Nicole offered over dinner one night. "Everything will be completed by then and the weather will still be lovely."

"I agree" added Jessie. "But Jake and I really don't want a big blown out affair."

"Neither do we" Matt added, but Nicole tossed him an evil stare. "Speak for yourself" she sniffed. "I have waited more years than I'd like to admit to for this perfect man to come along, and I would like the biggest celebration of the century."

"There goes the double wedding idea" Jake whispered into Jessie's ear. Matt gave Nicole a sidelong glance and stole a quick look at his best friend. This could be a problem, he thought. Matt hated the limelight and a huge wedding was the last thing he wanted. But he knew that if Nicole had her mind set on a big wedding, then that's what would be planned.

"So that's it then?" Jessie folded her arms across her chest. "No double wedding?"

"Fine" Nicole glared back at her.

"Because what Nicole wants, Nicole gets, right?" Jessie's eyes were burning right through Nicole's stare.

Jake and Matt glanced at each other, amused at the scene about to be played out. Both men hoped it wouldn't get out of hand. Neither relished the idea of carting their bride-to-be out of the restaurant.

"Jessie, I know most of your friends have four legs" Nicole bit through the air, "but Matt and I happen to have many friends who would love to share the happy day with us."

"Well let me tell you something" Jessie bolted forward in her seat. "My four-legged friends have more class"

"Okay" Jake jumped into the fray. "Let's not get ugly with each other."

Jessie slumped back in her seat and continued to glare at Nicole. The air had quickly become tense and Jake and Matt each raised their eyebrows.

Matt picked up the role of peacemaker. "I don't think we need to decide this right now. I'm sure there's a compromise in here somewhere. Let's just focus on a date for now."

"October" Nicole said, still glaring at her sister.

"Well if she's getting married in October," Jessie huffed, "I'm going to wait until spring."

Matt and Jake exchanged another quick glance, knowing they were witnessing sibling rivalry of monumental proportions.

"Look" Jake turned to Jessie "why don't we put this conversation away for now. You ladies can take some time to cool down and maybe find some middle ground when you're not so...." Jake searched for a word that wouldn't further incite the situation. "When you've had some time to think about it."

"I don't need to think about it" Nicole said as tears welled up in her eyes. "I've always dreamed of a big wedding."

Jessie rolled her eyes. "Here comes the drama" she murmured.

Tears streamed down Nicole's cheeks. "You're just being mean and selfish."

Jake touched Jessie's elbow. "Why don't we go for a walk."

"Fine" Jessie said as she slid from the booth. "I think" Jake cut in. "I'm not sure Nicole wants to hear what you think right now" he said as he escorted Jessie away from the table.

Nicole turned to Matt. "Do you see what I mean about

her? It's all about what she wants."

"Nicole" Matt started, but was taken in by Nicole's sad eyes. He slid his arm over her shoulder. "How about this...we have a small, quiet wedding and then after a few weeks we can have a huge party at the new house?"

"It's not the same."

"Why not? It could be a celebration of both the wedding and the new house?"

Nicole spun in her seat to face her future husband. "So will people bring us a nice crystal vase, or a nice shrub for the garden? No" she said, her eyes burning with new tears. "I'm not sharing my special day with a house because my sister doesn't know how to be social."

Matt tried a new approach. "What about what kind of wedding I want?" His arm tightened around her shoulder. "Do I get a vote?"

Nicole's lip began to quiver. "I would think you would want to see me happy."

She's good, Matt thought to himself. "Of course I want you to be happy, Nic, but we might all have to compromise a bit on this."

Nicole thought about this for a moment, then slid out of the booth and stood to look down at Matt. "I'll compromise on a lot of things," she said, "but my wedding day won't be one of them."

Matt shook his head as he watched Nicole walk away. He took money from his pocket, threw it on the table as he nodded to the waitress, and took after Nicole.

He caught up with her at the car. "Okay" he said as he took Nicole by the shoulders. "This isn't going to get resolved today. Let's forget about it for now and we can talk about it later."

Nicole twisted her shoulders from his touch. "There's nothing to resolve." She looked up as Jake and Jessie approached them.

"Nicole" Jessie said "Matt and I were talking, and we think we have the perfect solution."

Nicole raised her eyes but kept her silence.

"How about if we have the wedding together, but the reception is just for you and Matt?"

Nicole knitted her eyebrows. "You mean after the ceremony you two will just…leave?"

"Well, we would have a small, private reception at the house, and you and Matt could have your....celebration." Jessie tried to keep the last word from sounding like an admonishment.

"That doesn't seem like much fun" Nicole said. Her eyes suddenly lit up as the thought came to her. "How about this? You both come to the reception – everyone will be together – and stay through dinner. When the party starts, you two can head out if you want."

Matt and Jake glanced at each other, hoping this would be the final compromise.

Jessie looked at Jake who nodded his approval. "I guess that could work" Jessie said.

Nicole sprung forward and grabbed her sister. "I knew we would find a way to make it work." She gave Jessie an enthusiastic hug. Matt and Jake shook hands, relieved that the crisis was resolved with no blows exchanged between the sisters. They headed back to the beach house and celebrate their compromise with a cocktail hour.

As August slipped into September, Jessie had decided to let Nicole handle the lion's share of the wedding plans while she and Jake took care of the ranch and Matt kept the construction of the new house on track. They shopped for wedding gowns together, but outside of that the plans were left to Nicole. Jessie had to admit that part of the reason was to keep Nicole busy and out of her hair, but she also had to admit that as the wedding day grew closer she became more excited over the plans Nicole had made. The day was to be less extravagant than Jessie and Jake had feared. Nicole had planned an elegant but simple affair in Charleston for about 50 people and Jessie had to admit that Nicole's ideas were far better than anything she could have planned on her own.

As the Saturday in October dawned, Jessie and Nicole sat at the table in Jessie's kitchen.

"Where did Jake spend the night?" Nicole asked.

"At your new house with Matt. I think they had some of the guys over for drinks and poker." She shook her head and smiled. "Such a guy thing to do."

Nicole smiled "The furniture doesn't come until next week. I hope they brought sleeping bags."

Jessie smiled back but didn't respond. A silence filled the kitchen as the sisters were lost in their own thoughts.

Jessie finally broke into Nicole's thoughts. "So much has changed for us, hasn't it."

Nicole nodded, her thoughts still capturing her mind.

Jessie continued. "We lost our mother, but I found my daughter. You gave up your life in London but are starting a new life here. So much...." She let her words trail back into the silence.

"Jessie" Nicole finally started. "Today is the happiest day of my life but I feel sad."

Jessie's eyes followed Nicole's expression. "You're not getting cold feet are you?"

Nicole smirked at her sister's comment. "Of course not. But I was thinking last night that we were apart for so many years, then mother brought us together, and now we're going our separate ways again." She smiled as she looked into her sister's face. "It makes me kind of sad, that's all."

Jessie shook her head and teased her sister. "Nicole, you are the biggest drama queen I've ever met."

"Am not" Nicole countered playfully.

"We're going to be neighbors, for god's sake" Jessie laughed. "You can walk over anytime you feel the need for some sister bonding."

Nicole smiled then looked again at Jessie. "Do you think I'll be a good wife?"

Jessie recognized the true explanation for Nicole's mood. She isn't sad, Jessie thought, she's nervous. My sister is more nervous that I am.

"I think you'll be a terrific wife, Nicole. I mean, mother taught us some valuable lessons, didn't she? We can take those lessons of understanding and compassion and compromise and use them in our marriage. In our relationships with our husbands and our family."

Nicole watched Jessie as she spoke, nodding as the words became real to her.

Nicole stood and walked to where Jessie sat, and looked down at her sister. "I'm so glad I have you to remind me that I'm not a horrible wretch" she laughed half-heartedly.

Jessie stood and hugged her sister. "You're not a horrible anything."

The hall was already filled with friends when the limousines pulled up. Taylor had agreed to be the maid of honor for both of the sisters and Jessie's breath caught when she saw her daughter in a simple crème colored gown. Taylor hurried over to greet them as they stepped from the limousine, hugging Nicole first before she turned to Jessie.

"You look beautiful" Taylor said as she hugged Jessie and hooked her arm through hers. "I think I'm more nervous than you and Nicole" Taylor gushed. "Brian said if I'm this panicky as a maid-of-honor, I'll never make it as a bride."

Jessie stopped quickly and raised her eyebrows at her daughter.

"Oh, no, no, no" Taylor said, realizing what Jessie was thinking. "I didn't mean that Brian and I...we're not there yet."

Jessie nodded and continued walking toward the hall that Nicole had booked for the wedding and the reception. As they entered through the side door, the three women could hear the sound of glasses clinking and conversation among their friends.

Nicole reached for Jessie arm, stopping her as she entered the private room that had been set up for the brides. The sisters exchanged a look that was more telling than words.

This is it, their eyes said to each other. This is the day that mother wanted us to get to. She wasn't being mean or silly with her letters...she was making sure we were the best women we could be for ourselves and for the people in our lives that we love.

♥ ♥ ♥

42170625R00157

Made in the USA
Middletown, DE
11 April 2019